THE DARK BORDER

THE DARK BORDER

A WESTERN QUARTET

FRANK BONHAM
edited by Bill Pronzini

FIVE STAR

A part of Gale, Cengage Learning

GALE
CENGAGE Learning™

Detroit • New York • San Francisco • New Haven, Conn • Waterville, Maine • London

GALE
CENGAGE Learning˙

Set in 11 pt. Plantin.
Printed on permanent paper.

LIBRARY OF CONGRESS CATALOGING-IN-PUBLICATION DATA

Bonham, Frank.
  The dark border : a western quartet / by Frank Bonham; edited by Bill Pronzini. — 1st ed.
    p. cm.
  ISBN-13: 978-1-59414-741-8 (alk. paper)
  ISBN-10: 1-59414-741-8 (alk. paper)
  1. Western stories. I. Pronzini, Bill. II. Title.
PS3503.O4315D37 2009
813'.54—dc22   2008049389

First Edition. First Printing: March 2009.
Published in 2009 in conjunction with Golden West Literary Agency.

Printed in the United States of America
1 2 3 4 5 6 7 13 12 11 10 09

CONTENTS

FOREWORD

Born in Los Angeles in 1914, Frank Bonham determined at an early age that the written word would be his livelihood. He wrote his first short story at the age of ten, later studied journalism and worked on his high school newspaper, and made his first professional sale in 1935. That sale, of a mystery story to *Phantom Detective,* cemented his resolve to become a full-time fiction writer.

Late in 1936, he answered a newspaper advertisement placed by one of the legendary pulp writers of the era, Ed Earl Repp, for a "secretary-collaborator" (*i.e.* ghost writer). "In those days," Bonham once wrote, "I was prolific as a hamster, often producing a short story a day. For two years I had written fiercely—one hundred and thirteen stories, seven sales." He was given the job, and his three-year, bittersweet relationship with Repp hastened his learning of the craft of fiction writing and enabled him to become an unencumbered member of the pulp fraternity.

Two years of service in the U.S. Army (1942–43) interrupted his career, though he continued to produce stories when time permitted. From 1944 until the early 'Fifties, he contributed millions of words of Western and historical adventure fiction to a wide range of pulp magazine titles, among them *Blue Book, Dime Western, Star Western, Wild West Weekly, Lariat, Fifteen Western Tales, Action Stories, Argosy, Adventure,* and *Five-Novels.* Occasionally he placed a story in one of the slick-paper periodicals aimed at a much wider, nonspecialized audience, such as *Liberty,*

7

McCall's, and *Esquire.* Later, when he began producing such finely crafted Western novels as *Snaketrack* (1952), *Night Raid* (1954), and *Hardrock* (1958), his work also appeared in *The Saturday Evening Post* and *American Magazine.*

Overall Bonham's career spanned more than fifty years and the publication of several hundred short stories, eighteen Western novels, three mystery/suspense novels, and twenty-five young adult novels with such themes as deep-sea diving, drag racing, the supernatural, and life in the Chicano *barrios* of southern California. His final novel, *Eye of the Hunter,* one of his most accomplished Westerns, was published the year after his death in 1988.

Of his Western fiction, Bonham wrote: "I have tried to avoid the conventional cowboy story, but I think it was probably a mistake. That is like trying to avoid crime in writing a mystery book. I just happened to be more interested in stagecoaching, mining, railroading, *etc.*" This self-evaluation is a bit harsh. Bonham's interest in frontiersmen (and frontierswomen) other than cowboys—mustangers, miners, military personnel, freighters, stagecoach owners and drivers, riverboat captains, storekeepers, doctors, mountain men, fur traders, gamblers, rodeo performers, and many more—is what sets his work apart from the run-of-the-mill Western story.

This is the ninth collection of Bonham's western and historical short fiction to be published by Five Star Westerns, and the stories presented here, like those in the previous eight, demonstrate his diversity of theme, character, and setting. "Brand of the Bear Flag Mutineers" from *Star Western* (4/45) chronicles a bitter and bloody confrontation between U.S. soldiers and Secessionist troops in California's rugged San Bernardino Mountains during the Civil War. In "The Dark Border" from *Star Western* (8/48), a pair of adventurous cowmen win a hardscrabble ranch in a dice game in the south Texas badlands, and their subsequent involvement in the illegal running of cattle across the Mexican border leads to hard lessons learned for both. While many Western pulp writers portrayed Indians, blacks, Mexicans, and other minorities as stereotypical inferiors, Bonham generally adopted a much more realistic attitude toward ethnic groups; "Chivaree" from *Star Western* (4/51), whose central ingredient is the marriage of a white man and a half-breed Sioux woman, is one example. "Blood on the Bozeman Trail" from *Dime Western* (6/50) is the exciting tale of a freight-line owner beset by trouble from cut-throat competitors, Indian raiding parties, and other hazards during a trek along the Bozeman Trail from Cheyenne to the Montana border.

These stories, as with all of Frank Bonham's work, are superior traditional Western fare.

Bill Pronzini
Petaluma, California

★ ★ ★ ★ ★

Brand of the Bear Flag
Mutineers

★ ★ ★ ★ ★

I

Troop security had been John Drum's credo ever since he took out his first patrol as a cavalry shavetail. He entered no gap until his scouts had signaled it safe. On bivouac, he detailed pickets before ever a saddle came down.

This he had done tonight, when D Troop of the 4th California made dry camp at Old Woman Springs, under the blue tilts of the San Bernardino Mountains. Yet now, as the captain sat erect on his blanket, the thunder of hoofs rolled terrifyingly close, and over the dark rim of a hummock he saw horsemen pouring in a black wave. And no warning had been given.

The camp was awakening on a surge of panic. Corporal Foxen was at Drum's elbow, shouting: "Boots and Saddles, sir?" He was half dressed, bugle at his lips.

Drum said—"As skirmishers."—and buckled on his saber and seized his revolver in his left hand to run to where the horses were picketed. There was no time for saddling. No time for anything but a prayer and a man's stand.

1st Sergeant McCullah stood near the horses, looking as stern and firmly in hand as though this were a mere falling out for Reveille. Drum's courage lifted just for knowing he was here, a rock to lean on. A good man, McCullah, and a regular, like Drum himself. "I want three squads to guard the horses," Drum said. "Two others on each flank. The rest on the line."

Somewhere the lieutenants, Mirabeau and Kelsey, were bawling their men into formation. McCullah, tunicless, with his blue trousers outside his boots and his forage cap on the back of his square head, went running through the rows of mussed blankets. His commands came back to Captain Drum, imperative as pistol shots. Three corporals ran up with their men straggling behind, pulling on clothes and buckling sabers.

The night gave up a crackle of pistol shots and a picket cried out as Captain Drum deployed his men and himself crouched behind a spiny Joshua tree. Out of the formless gray-black wave materialized individual horsemen, riding back in the saddle, not on the withers, as good cavalrymen ride. To the captain's surprise only a handful carried sabers. These men rode straight at the horse-holders, the others charging the line.

Drum stood beside the tree, firing his revolver with the roar of it almost lost in the din. He saw two saddles empty. A thickset man veered toward him with his saber raised. An arm of the Joshua prevented his making the slash, and, while he swung the horse and lifted the blade for another try, Drum's long body went in close to the horse and he sent the point of his saber up under the man's ribs. He withdrew and felt the scalding flow of blood down his arm.

Not far off he heard Sergeant McCullah yelling. McCullah had made more noise than the rest of the squadron at Gaines Mill. "Now, you devils! Now, damn you!"

He had time to glance to his left. The men were holding, green, disillusioned volunteers from the gold fields that they were. Would they understand now why he had drilled them in the sun and put them on forced marches when there was not a Secesh troop within fifteen hundred miles? Would they understand that they were soldiers, that the legends of a Bear Flag Battalion had its roots in steel?

Captain Drum's first estimate had been of a force approximating a hundred. Now he realized they were much less than that. Those who had struck his center had fallen back, badly mauled by the pistol and carbine fire of his troops. They were swinging past the flanks, reaching for the safety of the night. Their force had been dissipated over a wide front instead of being hurled at one vulnerable spot.

Drum said to the bugler—"Boots and Saddles."—and was the first man to catch out his horse. Confidence came to him, a readiness for anything, the stimulus any good cavalryman took from the feel of a horse between his legs. McCullah swung in beside him to relay commands.

When the troops were all in line, mounted, Corporal Neff rode up. "Lieutenant Mirabeau is missing, sir."

Drum said: "Leave two men to find and care for him."

For an hour they searched the flat, arroyo-veined face of the desert. The attackers had broken ranks and spread far and wide. D Troop returned to count losses.

Four men were dead and six wounded. Three were missing, Lieutenant Mirabeau among them. Captain Drum took the report with a frown. After the wounded had been cared for, he wrote in his journal:

> *Attack was made tonight by a force of fifty horsemen, probably Bear Flaggers, intent on stealing our horses. Examination of papers on bodies shows no proof of affiliation with any Southern group. Lt. Mirabeau and two sentries are missing. Pickets had been posted but failed to give the alarm.*

He was too experienced an officer to confide any suspicions in his journal. He did not set down that he had distrusted Lieutenant Mirabeau, a militia officer, from the start. Nor did Drum add that he would have traded his whole troop for a squad of tobacco-chewing regulars such as he had led at Gaines Mill. But his reward for coming through that bloody hour alive had been to be singled out for a secret mission in California, leading a troop of inexperienced volunteers in search of the source of the Bear Flag organization, who were seeking to sever the Gold State from either the North or South, and form a Pacific Republic.

He closed the journal and lay back on his blanket, staring up at the black desert sky. By tomorrow night they would be encamped in Holcomb Valley, a mile high in the mountains. And by that time, in addition to his other troubles, he would have the nearness of a girl he had ridden away from three years ago to torment him. . . .

In the morning the men broke camp sullenly. "There's a lot of complainin'," Sergeant McCullah said. "They think they've earned a day's rest." He stood with his arms crossed, displeasure written in his roughly cut features. McCullah was a man who liked alacrity. He was also a man who got it, one way or another. He was over six feet tall in his blue uniform, a good load for any horse, and not an inch of fat under his belt.

"Speak to the NCOs," John Drum told him. "There won't be a man of them reënlist next month, but by Harry they'll all be soldiers by then!"

McCullah gave the non-coms the sharp edge of his Irish tongue and D Troop moved out in column. At 10:00 they made the gate of Van Dusen's Toll Road, an oasis of cottonwoods festooned with wild grape, its back against the barren foothills.

The eyes of Brown, the roadkeeper, shone when he saw the column of ninety-odd men with six wagons. "You go through the gate with my compliments, Cap'n," he said. "Sabers and bluecoats are what this road needs."

Drum leaned against the hoary cottonwood shading the road. He drank cold water from a gourd, his eyes closed. The captain was a man just under six feet, with the erect, hipless carriage of a cavalryman. The sun had put a dark stain in his skin, and in his gray eyes were mementoes of Gaines Mill and Yellow Tavern and a dozen other places where death had been only half the horror.

"Trouble?" he asked Brown.

Brown sat on his hunkers, making marks in the dust with a stick. "About a third of the freight that starts up the road don't make it to Belleville, in the Upper Holcomb. Wells, Fargo boxes coming out with bullion from the mines have been stolen."

"Do they bother the horses?" Drum asked.

"They're hoss greedy." Brown glanced up at him. "You want my opinion, Cap'n? Bear Flaggers! Hills are full of them. They're outfittin' troops somewhere."

"Is that just guessing?" Drum questioned sharply. "You couldn't mention any names or places?"

With the edge of the stick, Brown smoothed the marks he had made. He shook his head, smiling wryly. "Just guessin', Cap'n. Just guessin'."

It was in Drum's mind that the roadkeeper was afraid to say any more than he had. In things like this, men were often chary of talk. The column went on through the gate.

The toll road was a crude path hacked along steep mountainsides, now following a rocky wash, now winding along a windswept hogback. Through the first rank of dry hills they forged, crossing a deep cañon to mount the more rugged, timber-clad mountains that threw sharp barricades of granite two miles into the cloudless sky.

From sagebrush and Joshua the toll road carried them into denser stands of buckbrush, piñon, and cedar. The dry, heated air of the desert was a thousand feet below them; a coolness was in the atmosphere now. By night they were in the pine country and camp was made beside a small stream that crossed a wooded flat. In the morning they crossed a heavily timbered ridge and saw Holcomb Valley below them.

The valley formed a rough dog-leg, a stream traversing its

whole length. Drum could see the tawny scars of mine stopes and glory holes among the fragrant firs that timbered its enclosing hills. He could hear the rumble of an arrastre and the puff and clank of a steam engine crushing ore. Belleville, a neat pattern of log and adobe houses on the green meadow, occupied a loop of Holcomb Creek at the east end of the valley.

There was coolness and beauty and peace here, Drum saw. But for him there had been no peace for three years, and there would be none now. Not while a dark-haired girl had her fingers around his heart.

With Lieutenant Kelsey and the captain at the head, D Troop swung down through the shadowed aisles of giant trees and jogged onto the meadow. At the bank of the creek, Drum raised a gauntleted hand and said to Kelsey: "Take over, Lieutenant. I'll look up the mayor or whatever they have here and get permission to camp."

Kelsey saluted, a blond truculent young officer with long sideburns and no love for discipline. Kelsey's commission had been won through friends in the governor's office, but he had been soldiering for Drum.

Drum rode into town with no eagerness. The two letters he had received from Laurie during the last year had both been from Belleville. She might still be here, and she might not. He tried to hope that old George Owen would have packed his cobbling equipment and his daughter away to some other boom camp, but even though he knew the old wound would be reopened when he saw her, he would not have changed it.

It would be like this when he saw her, John Drum thought— both of them pleasant, smiling in the guarded way of those who hold their emotions firmly in their two hands. Both wanting each other and determined not to show it, for they had tried it before and there was no good in rehearsing all the old bitterness again.

He rode between the irregularly shaped buildings, no two of the same height or design. Men watched the upright blue figure on the sorrel horse jog past, not all with welcome in their eyes. It was a town of many interests and races, miners, *vaqueros,* and Chinamen mingling on the board sidewalks.

Drum smelled bread baking somewhere and heard the iron cry of a blacksmith's sledge as he passed a log smithy. Then everything else was forgotten when he saw the familiar, gilded boot swinging in the breeze before an unpainted adobe shop on his right. The board from which the boot swung was lettered: *G. Owen. Cobbling.*

Drum dismounted. He turned from looping the reins about a pole to see Laurie standing in the doorway, tall and slender in a high-bodied gown that fell gracefully from her waist. She put out her hands and he took them in his gloved ones, and it was not at all as he had imagined it would be. She did not smile. Her hair was a dark mass to set off the clear oval of her face, and her eyes looked at him as though she were seeing everything he had been since he had left her, as though she knew every thought he had had.

"You haven't changed," she said. "Not in three years. You're as hard and stubborn as you ever were. And as dissatisfied," she added firmly.

II

Drum drew off his gloves and he followed her into the shop. "You're wrong," he said. "I knew the Army was what I wanted. A man can make his plans and see them through. He can fight his enemies with their own weapons, on equal terms. It's not like Texas, Laurie."

The odor of food cooking in a back room drifted in to mix with the sour smell of leather. Dozens of pairs of boots hung from pegs in the mud wall behind a work bench.

They did not talk about Texas, nor about the plans they had built around the cattle ranch John Drum had hacked out of the brasada country in eight years of fighting border loopers and wild cattle. Drum had had enemies, as any man has who succeeds where others have failed, but they had smiled at him on the street and kept out of his way, except at night, when their hungry loops and running irons ate at his herds. It was Drum's outspokenness that had finally banded the little foxes into a murderous pack.

In a slavery country it was not popular to talk abolition. Drum did. So they came for him one night, masking their hatred with a cloak of politics, and, when they left, John Drum had a bullet in his shoulder, his buildings were a heap of smoking rubble, and his cattle had been run across the river into the thickets of Mexico.

That was when he grew sick of fighting in the dark. He could not justify himself by trying to kill every man he suspected of having raided him. He had not the heart to begin again, with no more prize, perhaps, than to lose it all over again. Laurie had told him he would never be satisfied to leave the fight unfinished; she would wait while he started over. But when a man has put too much of his heart into a thing, he has not enough left to begin again.

John Drum joined the Army a year before Fort Sumter. He knew now that he would not go back to civilian life, not even if it meant losing Laurie.

Drum said: "I was sorry when I was ordered to California, Laurie. Now that I'm here, I'm glad. It gives me one more chance to convince you that being an Army wife isn't much worse than being a cowman's wife."

With her hand Laurie pushed back a curl from her forehead; she let it linger there long enough for Drum to see the ring on her finger. "You're a little late this time," she said. "He's a miner. Dave Rockaway. We're going to be married next month."

Drum had felt the same coldness the night the Bear Flaggers attacked. His guard had been down, giving him no defense against the shock that struck at him. He covered it by frowning as he thrust his gloves under his belt. "You don't love him," he said.

Laurie was smiling, her quiet blue eyes amused. "Don't I? Didn't you know a woman ties a string to her heart when she gives it away?"

Drum could neither make a joke of it, nor smile at hers. "You didn't with me," he said. "You said you'd wait. I thought you meant it."

"But you wouldn't let me," Laurie protested. She looked at the ring. "He's handsome, John. And a rabid Abolitionist. You'll like him."

"I imagine," Drum said dryly, as steps sounded in the back room. Old George Owen, staring over the tops of square spectacles, stood in his leather apron with a dish towel over his shoulder. He exhibited no surprise at seeing the officer. He said: "*Hm!* Just in time, John. We're having venison."

Drum ate with them. The talk was about the war, but Drum's mind would not let go of what Laurie had told him.

They went back to the shop. Owen sat down at his bench, looking the captain over critically. "Lost weight," he remarked. "The desert?"

Drum shrugged. "I'll put it on again up here. We'll be here some time."

The cobbler brought his sharp hook knife around the toe of a boot, slicing off the excess leather. "Copperheads?" he said.

Captain Drum looked out into the bustling street, with wagons and horses passing constantly and miners in the rough, mud-caked clothing of their trade. He said: "No. Though there are plenty of them, too. I'm after some men who would rather

21

set themselves up as kings of a California Republic than fight for her as a state. My information is that they have their headquarters in the San Bernardinos."

George Owen turned the boot in his hands, squinting at it. "Better keep your eyes open," he warned. "Maybe just a little thing like this boot here will tell you something you want to know."

The remark rang oddly in the shop. Drum looked at the boot, which was a thoroughly worn black one badly stirrup-marked, but otherwise not unusual. "Meaning anything in particular?" he asked, somehow a bit annoyed.

Owen again began to trim. "Meaning that nobody will tell you much if he does know anything. We all know the Bear Flaggers are thick hereabouts. But nobody knows but what the man that shoes his horse is one, so we don't talk about 'em much. They do a lot of night work."

It was Drum's impression that Owen had meant something more specific than that, but the boot told him nothing. "Do you have a mayor?" Drum asked.

"You want Matt Harrower," George Owen said. He spat some tacks into his hand and began to pound with staccato bursts of the hammer. "Harrower sells mining supplies up the street."

Laurie went to the door with him; John Drum held her hand. It was a little stiff; it was not quite his, he knew, and knowing that hurt. "Then all I can offer you is my congratulations," he said. "But I'll be hoping this miner of yours goes booming off to some other camp."

Laurie said quietly: "If he does, I'll go with him."

Mayor Matt Harrower held forth in a large, barn-like store on the corner across from the tree in the road. The place was a conglomerate of every kind of implement a gold miner could conceivably employ to entice gold from the earth—rocker and pan and pick axe; bottles of *aqua regia* and iron rings to be sunk in concrete arrastres. A red door in the rear was lettered: *Explosives. Keep Out.*

Harrower sat on a tool box prying at his teeth with a gold toothpick. The mayor was a short, square-bodied man with a wide mouth like a bear-trap. He wore a corduroy jacket and corduroy pants tucked into lace boots.

He gave the officer a silent, assaying stare, then kept his eyes on him while he wiped the metal toothpick and replaced it in a tiny case. "Well?" he said.

Drum said: "I'm Captain Drum, commanding D Troop of the Fourth California. My orders are to encamp here until further notice. To make it official, I'd like to get your permission to camp on the meadow."

Harrower strolled to the door and gazed off across the rolling green meadow at the lines of tents going up. "Somebody tell you we needed help?" he asked.

"We didn't need to be told," Drum replied. "Belleville is notorious as a rendezvous for a lot of unwholesome elements."

Harrower smiled, showing him a line of wide-set teeth. "Well, some of the boys like to stir up a tempest in a teapot. Nothing serious. The boys at the mines are too busy to worry about politics."

"I don't suppose you would care to mention names?"

Harrower, not losing his smile, said: "I don't know that I would."

He was a man, Drum saw, who kept his guard up, a man who might know much, but would tell nothing deliberately.

"I'll need some lumber for a few temporary buildings," he said. "Is there a mill nearby?"

"There's the Mormon's Mill," the mayor told him, "run by Mormon Dowling. Don't let the name fool you, though. The Saints threw him out before they went back to Utah. Mormon will have a drink with you and take a chaw, then rob you on his lumber."

It was Drum's impression that Mayor Harrower's eyes, when he left the store, contained more of distrust than of friendliness, and more of concern than casualness.

III

When he reached camp, it was noon. The tents, a colony of dun pyramids on the light green grass, were all up and the stakes and poles were being dressed. Sergeant McCullah said: "These parlor pioneers will be the finish of me, Captain. It's a Gypsy camp this bivouac looks like."

"Any more complaining?" Drum asked.

The sergeant did not answer at first. "Yes, sir, some," he admitted after a moment. "I can't enforce an order without a fist behind it. With all respect to Lieutenant Kelsey, sir, he ain't much better than the men. I believe he has given Corporal Neff permission to bring you some grievance."

Drum's face did not change, but there was faint amusement in his eyes. "Send him to my tent," he said.

McCullah had had the captain's tent, larger than the rest, erected under a lone pine near the stream, at the end of the troop street. Lieutenant Kelsey's tent stood between it and that of the ranking non-com. Kelsey was sitting in the shade before his tent, writing a letter. He had his blouse off and his collar undone. When he saw the captain, he came to attention and made his salute.

"I don't think I heard Retreat sounded, Lieutenant," Drum said.

Kelsey's blue eyes could not mask his pique. He looked very young and very resentful. "No, sir," he said. "But a blouse gets hot."

"The uniform is dress until after Retreat," Drum said. And

then: "I have sent for Corporal Neff. I understand he has something on his mind."

Kelsey scowlingly got into his blue coat. It was in his face that he was finding soldiering under Captain Drum different from squiring the daughters of militia officers about the capital.

Corporal Neff appeared, a lanky, red-headed soldier with an aggressive chin and a small mouth made for cynicism. He wore the yellow chevrons on his sleeves without dignity.

Drum gave him at ease. "What's on your mind, Corporal?" he said.

Neff crossed his arms. He said: "Well, sir . . . most of us is plumb tired of soldierin'. It's all spit and polish, and hard work. On top of that, we ain't been paid in two months. What we want is our pay and a day or two off to spend it."

"You'll get it," Drum said quietly.

Neff's brows raised a trifle in surprise. But he saw the loophole in the statement and frowned. "Yes," he said, "but when?"

"Just as soon as the pay train gets through. While you wait, you'll continue to get Sundays off when there is no urgent reason to work. In the meantime, there will be drill every day, including today. I think some dismounted work wouldn't hurt anyone."

Neff's fists were agitated. "I don't know how the boys is going to take it."

The captain shrugged. "There will be discipline for anyone who finds the work tedious. Pass the word along, Corporal . . . and do it now."

When he had left, Drum spoke to Lieutenant Kelsey. "I'll leave McCullah to conduct drill," he said. "Take five men and ride to the mines. Get a gathering together here and there and see how many recruits you can bring back." Kelsey's fair skin, already sunburned and peeling, went redder, so that his sideburns and eyebrows stood out sharply. He pressed his lips together, then, without a word, turned on his heel, and went to saddle.

After lunch, Drum rode down the valley toward the sawmill. All the confidence he had spoken was not in him. These men he commanded were a stubborn, tired, and rebellious group of disillusioned volunteers, but their demand for pay was, of course, legitimate. However, until the paymaster's train came up from Fort Yuma, on the Colorado, there was not a penny to pay them. He was using government scrip himself for supplies and until the money came through there was nothing to do but keep them busy; busy men had not the time to grouse.

For a slightly different reason, Drum kept himself busy. He didn't like the intrigues that his job pointed at, and he didn't like inactivity. And he didn't like to think of Laurie, who had made it plain enough that any love that had been between them before had been buried long ago.

The Holcomb Creek trail carried him three miles west, the valley funneling down until it was a deep, ferned slot with slender stands of second-growth bull pine standing back from the edge of the creek. Where a rutted log trail descended from the mountain, the trail became a road, passing through sharply fragrant motes of manzanita and buckbrush. Over the tinkling voices of the creek Captain Drum picked out other sounds: a muley saw's protesting whine and the roar of a waterfall.

He came through the trees onto a bench where a sawmill and a handful of other log buildings stood in the slanting rays of the sun. A flume of whip-sawn logs carried the creek water from where Drum sat his pony to the top of a penstock about fifty feet high. Green water gushed from a gate in the bottom of the penstock to turn a ponderous undershot wheel. Drum watched two men with brown, bare backs feeding logs into the saw.

A voice near him said: "Looking for someone, soldier?" It

was a girl's voice. A voice with humor and warmth.

The girl lay on a great gray stone set in the hill, her chin resting on her linked fingers. Drum could see her upper body, slender as a young animal's. He could see her hair, bright gold, with a shining wash of copper. He had to stare for a moment; it was like seeing a scarlet tanager flash through the top branches of the somber trees on a gray afternoon. She raised herself on her elbows.

Drum said: "Why, yes. I'm looking for Mormon Dowling."

"Pop's in the office," the girl said. She slid down the rock and stood beside the trail, slim and brown-legged, with a wild, wanton sort of beauty. "I'm Selena Dowling. I'll take you inside."

Drum dismounted, introduced himself, and they walked to the mill. The girl smiled up at him. "What's the matter?" she said. "Are we fighting the war down here, now?"

"No," Drum answered soberly. "We're just making sure we don't have to."

Selena Dowling looked at him, from boots to forage cap, her eyes frankly admiring. "You Army men," she said. "Vain as peacocks! You had that uniform tailored, didn't you?"

Drum smiled. "The Army way, Miss Dowling, is to give a man a uniform and then tailor him to fit it."

They went up six steps to the sawing floor. Here the cry of the muley saw set Drum's nerves on edge, while the air was filled with floating particles of sawdust. The smell of hot pitch was a pleasant tang. They went into an office where a bear-like man sat at a desk counting yellowbacks. He scowled and shoved the money into a drawer.

"Seleny," he said, "don't be comin' in here without knocking. I've told you that."

The girl said: "Company, Pop. This is Captain Drum."

The Mormon looked at him without standing. He was a massive-shouldered, black-browed man with his vices written on his face. A preacher would have called it a face without a soul. Drum was not concerned with souls, but he could find no mercy for an antagonist in Mormon Dowling's small eyes or heavy-lipped mouth.

"What is it you want?" the Mormon said.

Drum gave him a slip of paper on which he had written the amount and description of the lumber he would need. With a stubby finger Dowling dug in his ear. "Is this cash?" he said.

Drum said: "Scrip. It will be redeemed within a few weeks."

The Mormon's eyes wandered up to his face. "I sell for cash."

Drum's jaw set. "This time you sell for scrip," he said. "I'll take the mill over if I have to."

Dowling made a mock gesture of assent, smiling one-sidedly. "Write out your scrip," he said.

Drum endorsed the draft and laid it on the desk. He said: "Another thing. I'm looking for some of my men who deserted a few days ago. Have you seen any other troopers recently?"

He saw a glance pass between the mill owner and his daughter, and he saw the Mormon's dark eyes barricade. But the girl said: "Three men?"

An electric eagerness went through the captain. "Yes. An officer and two privates," he said. "When were they through?"

Selena went on blithely, while her father pulled his brows down in disapproval. "Yesterday. They stopped and asked directions to Bear Valley." Her eyes sparkled. "A good-looking officer, Captain. Tall and dark, hadn't shaved, or he'd have been downright handsome."

"He was in too much of a hurry to shave. Deserters usually are. Did you show him the way?"

"I took them up to Marcos Pass Look-Out. That's only about two miles south, but it's straight up all the way."

Drum addressed his next remark to the Mormon. "I'd like to

ride up there for a look around. Can you spare a man as a guide?"

"I know the trails better than any of the loggers," Selena said. "I'll take you up."

"You'll stay here," said the Mormon curtly.

"There might be trouble," Drum agreed. "They're probably clear to San Bernardino by now, but just in case. . . ."

Selena opened the door, admitting the shriek of the saw and freshened odors of sawdust and pitch. "I'll saddle my pony!" she called back.

Mormon Dowling shoved the scrip roughly in the drawer. His faced showed anger, yet a rueful sort of amusement, too. "Damned little vixen," he said. "Wild as a catamount. But I reckon she can take keer of herself as well as any man."

They followed the log road for a mile, crossing a meadow blocked with fresh pine stumps that stood like stakes. The light mountain air carried the ring of axes from the still wooded section. Selena led across a creek and they started up the mountain trail. She had changed to denim pants, and she rode as easily as any cowhand.

Two miles, she had said. Most of it was along shelving ledges and slippery, tilted carpets of pine needles. They reached the Look-Out, a high saddle in the timber, where the wind combed the treetops with a soft, secret music and the vista was of blue ranges to the south, and then a great void where the valley lay, and farther still the pinkish bulk of San Gorgonio thrusting frostily into the sky.

"That notch is the pass," Selena said, pointing. "Bear Valley is eight miles from here." The wind's fingers were in her hair, and her eyes were bits of the sky's own blue. Many men might love her, Drum thought, but no man would ever own her. She was too wild; freedom was the very pulse of her.

Then his reflections were scattered, as something struck the rock beside him with a sharp, explosive sound. Drum had heard this sound before, thus he was rolling his spurs and driving against Selena's horse an instant before the *crack* of the rifle invaded the forest stillness.

IV

He sent the girl's pony *clattering* down the trail. He drew his carbine and swung from the saddle, giving the horse a single command. The animal lay down and remained rigidly still, while Drum sprawled in the space between head and chest and laid his rifle barrel across the sorrel's neck.

The scent of burned powder came to him. He noted the direction of the wind, and after this it was not difficult to locate the sniper. Directly before him, a hundred feet away, was a pile of moss-blackened boulders. Into a notch of this natural battlement he saw a gun muzzle thrust, a dark head rise behind it.

Drum knew the angry thoughts that would be in that treacherous head: disgust at having muffed the rifle shot, and at having now to resort to a pistol. He got the face behind the gun in the notch of his battle sights. He did not hurry the shot; the advantage now was his, and he would make it count. Steadily he took up trigger slack; just before the hammer fell another ball *thudded* against the earth and spat dirt over him. The dark head rose higher, studying, and Drum felt his own weapon thrust against his shoulder.

Selena, crouching behind a manzanita, cried out excitedly: "You got him!"

Drum said: "Stay where you are!" He changed swiftly to his .44. The sniper's revolver *clattered* down the rocks. There was no sign of the man, now, and, although the cavalryman waited several minutes, no other gunmen showed themselves.

Drum circled the rocks and saw the body lying crumpled in a cleft of the boulders. He was not surprised to find that the sniper wore the blue and yellow of the cavalry. Going closer, he discovered that it was Gorton, one of the deserters.

A high flame of eagerness mounted through him. If Gorton had been posted as sentry, Mirabeau and the other trooper would not be far off. It was Drum's thought that at this moment he was not more than a mile from the mountain rendezvous of the Bear Flag Battalion. Yet he did not dare go farther, if only for the sake of the girl. If there were any considerable organization to be reckoned with, it would not be moved far or fast before tomorrow.

He returned to the girl. "I'll take you back," he said. "The rest may be here before long."

She let him help her to the saddle, and he noticed that there was no pallor or trembling in her. She held his hand for a moment. "I like you, Captain," she said in her frank, open way. "I have never liked very many men."

Caught without an answer, Drum felt color flame into his face. He made himself busy for a moment with her latigo. "I suspect the reverse can't be said," he remarked. "I am sure many men have liked you. A rifle ball seems to be the way to your heart."

Selena laughed. "A gruesome way to put it," she said.

They rode back. Not far from the sawmill she let him pull in beside her. She gave him a direct, earnest glance. "Have you ever lived in a place like this?" she asked. "I mean, without anyone to talk to except a man who can't see beyond his cash drawer, and a crew of loggers without much space between the eyes?"

"I've lived in Army camps," Drum replied. "They aren't always what the recruiting sergeants tell you."

Selena's face showed an inner eagerness. "An Army camp would be like heaven compared to this," she told him. "A woman isn't young forever. And she can get old in a hurry. I remember my mother used to tell me that and I saw it work out, in her case. We followed Pop around to logging camps and mining camps and wild-horse trapping outfits. She married young. I guess she never went to a dance in her life. She died when I was twelve. I made a promise when she died, Captain . . . that I would see some of the world besides the backwoods. I still mean to keep it."

Drum looked at her, sensing the ferment within her, the pressure of youth seeking an outlet. "You will, Selena," he said. "You haven't the kind of spirit they can tie down. And when you get out, you'll have enough men around you to start an army of your own."

Selena stopped her pony under the branches of a black oak, facing him with eyes that had a challenge. "I don't want an army," she said. "Just the man I pick. Do you want to kiss me, Captain?"

Drum did. Not because he loved her, because he was too close to the hoyden spirit, the impulsive heart of her, to be concerned with anything so complex as love. She was a coquette, and it would have been the same with any man she took a fancy to, but it did not render her lips any less warm when Drum drew her toward him and brought her body tight against his.

They were both breathless after he released her. All the hunger of his love for Laurie had gone into that kiss, but when it was all over, he knew that hunger had not been satisfied even for a moment, for Laurie's lips had been between them.

When he left her at the Mormon's Mill, she watched him remount with a high color along her cheek bones. "You'll be back, Captain," she said.

Drum hesitated. "Yes," he said finally. "I'll be back." *If only with a posse for the deserters,* he thought. He didn't know how well his desire for her would wear after he was out of her sight. . . .

It was after nightfall when he returned to camp. 1st Sergeant McCullah was waiting at his tent with a cigarette in his lips that he threw down and tromped out as the captain dismounted. Drum had noticed the strange lack of activity about the camp. McCullah's stony face told him there was trouble. "Where are the men?" Drum asked him.

McCullah's jaw muscles worked. "In town, sir," he said. "I took roll call an hour ago and there's twenty-four missing. Lieutenant Kelsey ain't back yet. I told them there would be company punishment for any that left camp."

Drum struck his gloved hands together. He began to smile. "Do you reckon two old Army men are as good as twenty-four volunteers, McCullah?" he said.

When McCullah grinned, it was like ice breaking up; his dark skin folded into many wrinkles and his eyes and his even teeth flashed. "I'll saddle and be right with you, Captain," he said.

Belleville possessed many saloons, but only one Hollow Log. An immense section of pine log, a door cut in the heart of it, made a woody halo about the entrance. Inside, yellowing pine boughs framed every door and window. The light came from lamps roosting about the rims of horizontally suspended wagon wheels.

Drum and the sergeant stood in the doorway. The bar of the Hollow Log was a solid rank of blue. Here and there at gaming tables sat a trooper or two; a few more men of the 4th California moved about the dancing area in back, with the bar girls. Mayor Matt Harrower, his bear-trap mouth full of laughter, had his arms about the shoulders of Corporal Neff and Corporal Foxen, the bugler.

Drum said to the 1st sergeant: "Bring Foxen over here."

McCullah spoke to the bugler, who reared back and swore in his face. The mayor made pacifying gestures with his hands, but Sergeant McCullah stepped up to Foxen and brought his fist up, almost gently, under his jaw. He caught the sagging body and half carried it to the door. Matt Harrower came along. No one but a few men at the bar had seen it happen.

Foxen looked angry and undecided when he saw the captain. Harrower tucked his thumbs in his vest pockets. "Aren't you being a little hard on the boys, Captain?" he said. "A little likker lubricates the joints."

"It also disgraces the uniform and leaves the camp unprotected," said Drum flatly. "Sound Assembly, Corporal."

Foxen, his eyes rebellious, unslung the bugle and blew the call, the sharp brassy sounds cleaving the mix of saloon noises. Every man in the saloon, and a dozen spangled beauties, stared at the quartet by the door.

Drum said: "You've got five minutes to finish your drinking and fall in by the pine tree." As he turned to go, he heard Corporal Neff's voice.

"Maybe we ain't finished, Captain. What about that?"

What Neff did, the captain knew, would be a pattern for the conduct of the rest. He walked down the bar and stopped before him.

"Well, if you're sure you aren't ready," he said, "we might as well settle it right now. Peel off, mister."

He removed his own saber, revolver, and tunic, and laid them on the bar. The redhead, moving with jerky eagerness, followed suit. He faced the captain, his fists knotted, but still hanging at his sides. To Drum, there was a fantastic side to it. The War Department would have demanded his commission in an hour if his brawling with an enlisted man in a saloon were ever reported. But the portent of this moment went deeper than the customs of the service. The valley was a serpent that wanted only a touch to come to life. While it lay dormant, Drum could lay his traps. Once aroused, it would be too late. A challenge like Neff's could be the impetus to wake the sleeping fangs.

Neff stepped in fast, driving for the captain's face. Drum tilted his head and the fist slipped past; he gave Neff a short jab to the stomach. The corporal grunted, backing away. Drum did not follow him. He counted on the enlisted man's temper matching his hair; an angry opponent was always a floundering one.

With some discretion, Corporal Neff advanced again, keeping his guard up this time. Drum feinted at his stomach, and, when the big, freckled fists dropped, he found Neff's nose with a stinging left. Now the corporal was bleeding and hurt and filled with rage. He moved in without caution, swinging savage roundhouse blows.

Captain Drum took them on his shoulders, his forearms. He let the trooper swing until he was winded, now and then slashing, short and hard, through an opening. Neff slowed down; his breath labored through swollen lips. And then Drum went to work.

A cracking blow over the eye stunned the man and stood him up like a target. Drum threw a hard one against his jaw, following it instantly with a driving blow to the mouth that sent Neff stumbling down the bar. Drum followed, hooking, jabbing, cutting the horsey face until the blood splattered as he landed each telling blow. There was a stricken look in the corporal's face now. He was finished, but he could not fall. Drum sank a fist in his stomach that doubled him up, then slugged him on the jaw. Neff went down, a bloody blue pattern against the tawny sawdust.

Drum put on his tunic and walked out without a glance back. And as he went, carrying his equipment, he heard them following him.

V

In the morning a courier from Fort Yuma rode in on a gaunt-looking mount. Drum read the letter he carried and was relieved to learn that the government pay train would make rendezvous with them in Bear Valley in two days. But at the same time he was worried. They were too close to the Bear Flaggers' hideout. There was small chance of cutting sign on the rebels before the rendezvous, unless Mirabeau's trail led him to their stronghold. He was deciding how many men he could afford to take with him when Lieutenant Kelsey appeared with a group of six miners. The officer seemed crestfallen. "Recruits, Captain," Kelsey announced. "I covered most of the diggings, but we don't seem to be popular."

Drum swore them in and sent them off in charge of a noncom to draw equipment. Then he called back one of the men to whom he had given the oath. "Did you say your man was Rockaway?" he asked.

The man grinned. He was a young fellow with blond hair and friendly brown eyes, a jaw like a saddle horn and a big man's fists. He nodded. "I got tired of shoveling gold out of the hills while other men are shoveling trenches. Think we'll see any action?"

"Liable to," Drum said. Then he said: "You're engaged to Laurie Owen, aren't you?"

Rockaway grinned. "That's right. You must have liked the Army, Captain, to have given her up."

"So she told you," Drum said. "This puts us both in an embarrassing position, Rockaway. I don't make a secret of the fact that I'd still marry Laurie if she'd have me. Perhaps I should have you transferred to Pennsylvania."

Rockaway shrugged. "I joined up to fight. But if you transfer me, I don't think it will be for revenge."

Drum walked toward the quartermaster's tent with him. "If

you know these hills," he said, "I can put you to work right away. I found proof yesterday that two men who deserted in the desert are hiding near Bear Valley. We're taking their trail this morning."

"I've spent ten years up here," Rockaway said. "I can take you to every cave and cañon big enough to hide a jack rabbit."

John Drum watched him join the men getting outfitted. *A well set-up lad*, he thought, *with the makings of a good soldier.* He sighed. It would have pleased him to have been able to suspect Dave Rockaway of sedition. Admiration was the last thing he wanted to feel for a rival.

While he was waiting for the detail to form, Laurie Owen came rattling down the creek road in a buggy. She stopped by his tent. She was smiling, but he saw soberness behind her eyes.

"So you've stolen my fiancé," she said. "I didn't think you'd misuse your power this way, John."

"I tried to talk him out of it," Drum told her. "Now that he's in, I won't have to worry about running into him when I go courting. I thought you'd've given him back his ring for joining, though. I remember once before when you did that to a man."

His irony did not disconcert her. "This was patriotism," she said. "The other time it was . . . running away." Then she changed the subject, indicating a pile of boots in the space behind the seat. "I'm taking these down to the Mormon's. Those loggers go through a pair of soles in a month. If you have any to be repaired, I'll pick them up on the way back."

Drum chuckled. "I may have a few pairs, at that." He noticed a high black knee boot on the top of the pile, and his smile faded. "That's a cavalry boot," he said sharply. "Does that go to the sawmill?"

Laurie said quietly: "That's the real reason I stopped here. Look at it."

Drum picked up the boot, which had seen hard wear but had

thick, new soles. He glanced inside, near the top, and what he saw made his heart strike his ribs. The boot was marked: *Anthony R. Mirabeau, Lt. 4th Calif. Cav.*

"Dad tried to tell you the other day," Laurie said. "He used to talk Union all the time, until a couple of fires were started in the shop at night that cost us six months' profit. We knew it would be a bullet the next time." She looked at the heap of mended boots. "Those don't all belong to loggers. The Mormon sends up a half dozen pairs a week. He's only got fifteen men on his payroll. Most of the boots are miners'. Someone is drilling troops in these hills. And I think the Mormon knows who . . . and where."

"You don't think it's Mormon Dowling?"

"Dad and I think that Matt Harrower is the kingpin. It would logically be a man who knows all the undercurrents he has to reckon with. And that would mean the mayor."

Drum stood there with the boot in his hand, thinking that as small a thing as this could make or break a revolution, that if he could follow this clue down to its source, he could destroy the Bear Flag movement before it went any further. But if Mirabeau got his troops out of the San Bernardinos and began to prey on the stage and freight lines from Los Angeles, a hundred other secret organizations would rush to join him. And then, with the supply line two thousand miles long, across the Seven Deserts of the territory, it might be too late to beat out the flames of revolt.

He threw the boot back into the buggy. "I'll take a few men and deliver these for you," he said. "I don't like to spoil a good customer, but we may be throwing some business in the way of the undertaker before we're through."

He had the boots loaded onto a pack animal. With fifteen men, he started for the sawmill. He had picked his men, McCullah and the best rifle shots in the troop, for if there were a battle, it would likely be a forest skirmish where sabers would be almost useless.

They rode down the river, feeling the coolness and moisture of the air on their skin. Some distance short of the mill, Drum called a halt. He looked at the faces of the men; they were surly and stubborn, but deeper than that he saw the beginnings of confidence in themselves and their weapons. They would never believe that the endless drilling they had undergone had made something like soldiers out of them, but when they came face to face with slaughter and exhaustion, they would stand up like men, and marvel at their own courage.

"I'll go on alone," Drum told McCullah. "If the Mormon sees a gang like this, he may fight on general principles. I don't know how many men we have to reckon with, but, if I can get inside, I may be able to find out what we want to know without a scrap. Give me five minutes, then attack."

He jogged boldly into the mill yard, between piles of fresh-sawn planks. The undershot wheel sent up its creaking and the saw screamed monotonously, just as though there were nothing to differentiate this mill from any other. As he dismounted, he saw the Mormon standing on the sawing floor. The mill owner stood at the top of the steps, and Drum stopped a step below him. In the Mormon's piggish eyes could be read anything—warning, or anger, or native sullenness.

"The lumber goes out tomorrow," he said. "That what you came for?"

Selena came to stand behind her father. The same tension was in her face that filled the sawmill. The four men at the saw table had stopped to watch.

Drum said: "It appears we'll be here longer than I thought. My instructions are to put up permanent barracks. It will mean a big order. Suppose we go inside and talk prices."

Selena's eyes were saying: *No!* But her attitude was casual as she stood there with one hand on her hip.

"We can talk about it here," the Mormon said.

Drum spoke impatiently. "We'll both lose our voices if we try to shout over that saw any longer."

Mormon Dowling's bulky shoulders moved carelessly, then he turned and led the way toward the office.

Selena Dowling walked beside the trooper. "Are you crazy?" she whispered. "Mirabeau is in there. He came back last night. He'll kill you."

Drum said: "Get out of here. There may be shooting."

The Mormon passed through the door first and just before Drum entered the room Selena's slender body thrust itself in front of him. Thus the lean, dark man in cavalry blues who sat behind the desk held his fire for an instant. Mirabeau had just shaved; his jaws were still shining from the touch of the razor, and his small mustache was a clean, black line. Suave and cynical and dangerous—that was Mirabeau.

Drum's gun was already out, but he was not prepared for the pair who leaped upon him from either side of the door.

He went down loosely, feeling the brutal impact of a gun barrel against his head, Selena's scream hammering against his ears.

He had a memory of many men moving through the room, of shots and angry cries. Then there was silence, until the shock of icy water brought him back to consciousness.

McCullah had loosened his collar, was holding a dipper of water near his face while he tried to sit up. John Drum drank some of the water before he said: "Outflanked, McCullah. They got away?"

"The Mormon, Mirabeau, and two others," answered the sergeant. "They made it across the flume before we realized what was happening. Their horses were tethered in the brush. We dropped three of the loggers."

Full recollection came back to Drum, like a fist around his heart. He said: "The girl?"

The sergeant closed one eye and made a clucking sound. "Game as a catamount. She dived out the window when the shooting started and waited for us. She took the boys on up the hill after them. What trails she don't know, Rockaway may."

But when the troopers returned, it was without encouragement. Drum left two men at the mill to stand watch. Selena Dowling stayed with them, confident that the Mormon and his cronies would not return.

As they started off, Dave Rockaway looked back once. "Plucky little devil," he said. "Knows these hills better than I do. And ain't afraid to ride 'em."

Looking at him, Drum had a thought that was not entirely scrupulous. Perhaps Rockaway's interest in her could be helped along a little—a few passes, sentry duty at the mill, and the like. . . .

VI

It was near sundown when they returned, but Laurie was still there with the buggy. Drum drove her back to town. She was full of curiosity about the skirmish at the sawmill, but her questions did not come until they were rattling up the road. Drum felt her gaze on him as he drove.

"There's a cut on your forehead," she remarked. "Was there a fight?"

Drum told her about it. "Aren't you interested in how Dave Rockaway came out?" he asked. He was smiling, and the color spread out quickly on her cheeks.

She said tartly: "Of course! I supposed he was all right, or you'd have said so."

"He's fine," Drum told her. "He spent most of the afternoon riding around with Selena Dowling. They seem to hit it off

41

pretty well. But then, any man would get along with Selena."

Laurie made an almost imperceptible sniffing sound. "You know, you didn't have to drive me back to town, if there was anything else you'd rather be doing."

Drum said: "I'm going in on business. The boot thing of yours has begun to work into something big. I'm going to talk to Harrower."

He left her at the shop and walked into the early night, full of optimism. Of one thing he was sure. Laurie had taken Dave Rockaway on the rebound. Whether or not her loyalty would make her go on with the marriage was another matter. . . .

Matt Harrower's living quarters were behind the shop where he sold mining equipment. When there was no answer to Drum's knock, no gleam of light in the dark building, the cavalryman walked down an alley and approached the store from the rear. He held a match to the window and could make out the foggy outlines of a table, a chair, and a cot. But it was the stout, steel-banded trunk in one corner that held Drum's interest.

A stout brass padlock on the door blocked entrance that way, and Drum inspected the casing of the window. It was the usual wood and adobe proposition: a frame of one-inch lumber mortared into the opening with mud plaster. Drum went to work with a knife. Ten minutes was all he required to scrape away enough mud to loosen the whole casing. He crawled into the room.

Now, as he stood in the small room, sorting the impressions that came to him, sounds reached him; the room was dark and cold as a cellar, smelling of stale coffee and dirty linen. Drum lighted a candle.

The trunk was locked. He brought an eight-pound maul from the front and smashed the hasp loose. Then he went swiftly through the trunk, finding nothing but clothing and a few old books.

Drum remembered now the red door in the main room, the one with the sign reading: *Explosives. Keep Out.*

It took longer to break into this compartment. After he had smashed the padlock to pieces, Drum stood and listened. Only dim sounds from the saloon, a faint singing and the muted *clatter* of glassware, came to him. He went inside and shut the door, then carefully struck a match. At the same instant, his breath caught.

The cubicle was only a blind. Along the walls were ranged kegs of black powder and coils of fuse. In the center of the dirt floor was an open trap door with stairs leading away into blackness. As he stood there, Drum heard a sound.

Just a whisper, the faintest *tinkle* of a spur rowel, but Drum knew that nothing moves so lightly as death. The cellar opening was suddenly a doorway to hell. Men were down there; he didn't know how many; there was a way, possibly, to tell. He extinguished the candle and rolled a powder keg to the top of the stairs; with a shove he sent it thundering down into blackness, then followed swiftly after it.

A man shouted profanely. Someone cried out, and there was the room-trapped sound of a shot. Silence came then, until a man said cautiously: "Matt?" It was the nasal voice of Corporal Neff.

"Right here," Mayor Matt Harrower growled. "I think he slipped on the stairs. The light went out and down he come. Reckon I got him."

Rusty metal scraped, and across the blackness drove the startling beam of a hurricane lantern. Drum saw the two men staring down at the splintered keg. A table stood behind them, and there were maps on the wall, as well as a flag showing a brown bear on a white background. Drum stepped from the

43

stairway into the room.

"All right, boys," he announced quietly. "The Army's moving in now."

Neff dropped the hood of the lantern and reached for his gun just as darkness rushed into the cellar. Drum fired once and moved quickly from the spot. There was no sign from the corporal, not until a Colt blasted into the blackness, and then Neff and Harrower began to move frantically. Drum knew the rush would be for the stairs. He sent a shot where he reckoned the redhead would be; in the brief flash he saw him break stride and twist spasmodically, trying to claw at his back.

He heard Harrower plunging up the stairs. When he moved to follow him, four shots came in staccato from the top. Drum heard the door of the dynamite room bang open. He ascended cautiously. The store was soundless when he gained the top. He went out into the alley, but there was no trace of Harrower, no sign that the gunfight had been heard by other ears. Drum knew the futility of trying to scare up a posse to hunt his man down. It would be better to scour the cellar stronghold now and form his own posse later.

Neff was dying when he returned to place the lamp on the table. He was breathing in a snoring fashion, his mouth streaming blood. Horror was no novelty to Drum; he ignored the dying man while he made a quick inspection of the room.

On the wall were colored maps of various sections of the state, showing in red all the stage and freight trails. Black stars along these routes could have meant anything; Drum's notion was that they indicated vulnerable points to be struck when the Bear Flaggers were ready. In a wooden box against the wall he found the correspondence of the Bear Flag outfit. As he riffled through it, he realized that all the tangled life lines of the organization, from San Diego to the Oregon border, had their source in this cellar.

The letters were all addressed to *Mayor Matt Harrower.* Many were terse, ungrammatical scrawls: *We got twenty-five men drilling now. Carbine for each and six sabers for outfit. Talking about combining with the Santa Barbara outfit. Would this be all right?*

In another receptacle, a tin strongbox, were onion-skin letterpress copies of organization rosters. A glance showed Drum that the Bear Flag Battalion numbered something over a thousand. Who knew how many other thousands would be drawn to this wild-eyed core, like filings to a magnet, when the rebels took the field? Drum paid special attention to the Holcomb Valley roster. He counted seventy-six names, including those of Mormon Dowling and Lieutenant Mirabeau.

With his search completed, he noticed a much-folded sheet of yellow paper lying on the table where the two men had sat. He read it, scanning again the words that the courier from Fort Yuma had brought him. Neat, traditional phrases that had the force of a thousand bugles: *Government pay train consisting of one officer and twelve enlisted men . . . proceed to a point known as Marble Rock . . . to make contact not later than July 26. . . .* July 26! The detail bringing the gold would be somewhere on the Green Cañon trail now, riding into whatever ambush the Mormon and Mirabeau had prepared for them. Drum had carried the dispatch with him, intending to destroy it. He had not had time, however, because the Mormon had removed it from his pocket while he was unconscious.

An hour ago there had been no hurry to make contact with the train. A four-hour ride in the morning would have brought them to Marble Rock, at the head of Green Cañon. Now it was clear that they must ride like fools to head off Mirabeau's party.

VII

It was an hour before Drum made it back to camp. He awoke Sergeant McCullah and Lieutenant Kelsey and ordered them both to his tent in fifteen minutes. He gave Foxen, the bugler, the order for Boots and Saddles. Foxen gave him an incredulous stare, as if wondering whether this martinet did not know that a night detail, with the men in their present rebellious mood, might be the last pound of pressure to cause an explosion.

In his tent, Drum showed Kelsey and McCullah what he had brought from Harrower's cellar. "It's the real thing this time," he said. "Matt Harrower jerks the wires for all of California. He's jerked them this time to intercept our pay train in Green Cañon. If they reach them before we do, we've lost doubly . . . they've got gold to operate on and we've lost whatever chance we still have to hold D Troop together."

Kelsey's still sleepy eyes were sardonic. "Does the captain think any of the men will reënlist?" he asked.

Drum regarded Kelsey carefully, noting the bored manner, the petulant mouth. "You're very young, Lieutenant," he said. "Very young and very inexperienced." He said, as if changing the subject: "Have you ever seen a man decapitated by a saber?"

Kelsey's eyes flinched.

Drum drew his sword and turned the bright blade in his hands. "Sometime tonight or tomorrow morning you'll see how one of these looks when it's running with blood. If you're lucky, you'll learn how it feels when it passes through bone. If you're not, you'll learn the other lesson. You and the rest of my pea-green command will find out about horror and fear. Dying men make ghastly sounds. They get under your horse's feet and scream when they are stepped on. But you keep on swinging, because you're fighting for your life. You've forgotten all about strategy and plans of attack, but you fight like a madman, cutting your way through a wall of flesh, and, when you break through, you realize suddenly that you've carried out your plan. The enemy is yours. Do you know why you've succeeded, even after you forgot everything but how much you wanted to live?"

Kelsey only stared, his jaw hanging. "Because a man you hated made you drill in the sun," Drum continued relentlessly. "Because he woke you up on a score of nights and made you ride around officering resentful troopers. He made you take so many imaginary enemies that when you came up against a real one you did it automatically." Suddenly Drum smiled, a little pityingly. The lieutenant's face was waxy. He said: "I'm sorry if I've been crude, Mister Kelsey. But I want you to know what you're going into. And I want to hear you swear at your men and threaten them and saber the first who turns back. Afterward, I'll join you in praising them."

Kelsey said—"Yes, sir."—and went outside, forgetting to salute. They heard him pause on the walk, getting a deep breath of cool air.

Drum had a pint of brandy in his portmanteau. He poured two inches in a tin cup and handed it to 1st Sergeant McCullah. "Gaines Mill, Sergeant," he said.

"Gaines Mill," the Irishman said. They drank the brandy. "And don't worry about the men," McCullah said. "No outfit that can complain so much can be too short on fight."

D Troop formed resentfully on the drill field, sabers *clanking*, horses snorting in the crisp mountain air. Drum sat his horse, his commands coming with a hard ring. He watched the men swing into the saddle. They faced him in silence, their faces lighter patches along the dark line. There was hate in those faces, but in a few hours there would be so much fear in them that they would have no room for hate. Then they would either hold, because he had made them strong, or they would break, because he had failed.

His voice went sharply through the night: "Right by twos . . . ho!"

The going was swift on the meadows, but when they swung up the Marcos Pass trail caution was the order. He sent Rockaway and a non-com ahead to smell out traps. About midnight a cold slice of moon rose over the hills to filter a wan light through the trees. The pines stood starkly menacing as they worked upward toward Marcos Pass. It was cold; the men had their tunics buttoned high and their gauntlets pulled up over their cuffs.

They halted for a ten minute break in the high gap known as Marcos Pass. Below them, Bear Valley was a dark, echoing void, full of the whisper of moving waters. Miles to the right a notch in the chain of timbered peaks showed where Green Cañon cut toward the desert, a two days' ride west.

A pre-dawn grayness was in the east by the time they reached the valley floor. Rockaway came back with the other scout from Marble Rock. He gave his report with subdued excitement.

"We raised 'em in the cañon below the rock," he announced. "There's lights along both sides of the cañon where they're smoking. They haven't been soldiering long enough to learn about giving away their position."

"Any chance for a frontal attack?" Drum asked him.

Rockaway shook his head, making a sketch in the dirt. "The cañon is straight up and down. They're deployed along a hundred-foot front. If we attack on this side of the cañon, we'll run into crossfire from the other side. I'd advise sending a detail across to the other side to strike at the same time we hit them. It's chancy, though."

Drum said: "That's the way the Eighteenth did it at Hunt's Ferry. Does fighting come natural to you?"

Rockaway grinned. "I fought the Kaws under Major Hastings for two years. That was six years ago."

"You got out before the war, though."

Rockaway said: "You bet. I didn't mind the fighting so much. But I hate the spit and polish, and fifteen dollars a month isn't much for working like a pit mule."

In the gloom, Drum looked at him. This man hated the Army, and yet he had joined again. He had given up Laurie, perhaps, and his stake in a gold boom that couldn't last forever, to risk his life. It made it a little painful to think of his own reason for joining. . . .

Near the head of Green Cañon, Drum split his command. He said to Lieutenant Kelsey: "Take your men across here and time it to attack in a half hour. The bugle will be the signal. Allow yourself some leeway, in case the pay train should come through sooner. And watch out for traps. Mirabeau is no fool."

Drum took his command along the narrow mountain trail on the precipitous north wall of Green Cañon. The river brawled in the grayness far below, sending up its moist coolness. Suddenly Rockaway spoke to Drum.

"They're directly below us, Captain."

Drum picked out the skirmish line that Rockaway's finger indicated, perhaps a quarter mile below them in the rocky bed of the cañon. There was little to indicate where the Bear Flaggers lay, except an occasional movement of man or horse. The animals were tethered back in the pines on the steep hillside; the ambuscaders had their positions in a fringe of willows along the river road.

The situation was ideal—mounted troops against dismounted. Drum's pulse quickened. He consulted his watch. Twenty minutes since he had left Kelsey. If they could remain undiscovered until Kelsey had had time to take up his position, they could crush Mirabeau's force with one stroke.

Sergeant McCullah rode along the line, talking to the tight-lipped non-coms. He gave them nothing but irony and censure, but the men he spoke to somehow sat a little straighter after it. McCullah stopped near the captain to scan the cañon as the first spears of daylight struck the tops of the trees. He stared, his body rigid.

"Captain," he said, "look there."

Drum's first warning was the *tinkle* of a harness bell. Then he saw what the sergeant had indicated—a little line of pack animals and a dozen blue-coated troopers riding into the ambush. . . .

Now there was no time to wait for Kelsey, no time for anything but shouting the charge and plunging down the slope at the head of the line. Foxen pulled in beside him; halfway down Drum gave him the signal to sound the charge for Kelsey—if Kelsey could possibly be within a mile of the battlefield.

Below them, startled men were pouring out of the willows and running for their mounts. The horse holders fought the excited ponies while the rebels tried to mount. And now rifle fire broke from the trees across the river. Over there other men were leaving their carefully selected vantage points to mount and meet Drum's charge.

Among the miscellany of miner's rigs and nondescript attire one uniform stood out—Mirabeau's, as he whipped his men into formation. Across the river another skirmish line was forming, the Mormon's voice coming hoarsely. There would be no surprise now, no quick victory. Every foot they won would be at a cost.

Drum glanced along the surging, sliding line to each side of him. The men of D Troop were too busy avoiding falls to worry about what lay ahead. But as they hit the flat above the road, the Bear Flaggers came out in a wide spearhead, and sabers came up with one impulse.

They tangled, the blue tide and the patchwork, but it was the blue that plunged on. The men were yelling, sabers bloody, tasting the strong brandy of victory. Anxiety struck at Drum. It had been too easy; the line had given way in the middle like a rotten core. And there was still no sign of Kelsey's detail. They were badly outnumbered, and suddenly he saw Mirabeau's strategy. It would not have worked, with Lieutenant Kelsey as a diverting force. But Kelsey was not there. Drum was confronting the Mormon and his band, splashing across the river to tangle with them, and he was flanked on each end by the two segments of Mirabeau's broken line.

He shouted at McCullah: "Deploy three squads in the rocks to hold Mirabeau! I'll take the Mormon."

He met the Mormon's forty-man thrust with twenty sabers. Drum picked out the bearish man's red plaid shirt and met him in mid-river, half-standing in the stirrups with his saber out across the head of his mount. There was no sureness in the way Mormon Dowling charged him, waving his sword like a flag. The blade came down like a guillotine at the top of Drum's head.

It was the easiest parry of all. Drum's blade tipped up and slipped the force of the Mormon's stroke. His saber came down again, finding the soft flesh under his opponent's collar bone. The blade sank in to the hilt, so that the force of Drum's charge hurled his victim from the saddle.

As he wheeled now to pick out another, he saw things that made him proud of these rebellious parade-ground soldiers of his. They were not throwing away an inch. They were dug in like bulldogs, sabering, swearing, emptying their pistols with their left hands, as he had taught them to do. But they were falling, too, borne down by superior numbers.

Back in the willows, McCullah and his men were on their knees, mangling Mirabeau's troopers with their accurate fire. They had tried a rush and been thrown back. Now they were packing in closer for a charge that must succeed by sheer weight and daring.

Drum saw it coming. He wished there were some way he could tell these men that he was proud of them—that at last they were the soldiers he had tried to make of them, and that they were not being slaughtered because of any fault of theirs. A laggard officer who had, perhaps, deliberately delayed his charge was responsible for that.

He heard McCullah roar a fire order, and knew as he turned back to meet a rebel's charge that Mirabeau was coming through. And then he heard another voice—a high-pitched voice without much confidence in it, but stiffened, somehow, with determination. Kelsey was here. Kelsey, who had thought to fight the war in the drawing rooms of Sacramento, was throwing his men against Mirabeau's!

Mirabeau swerved, confused, and 1st Sergeant McCullah called up the horse holders and remounted his men. He struck at the dark-faced deserter from the left flank, so that Kelsey was able to draw off half his platoon to go to Drum's aid. The blond lieutenant had blood on him. He had lost his forage cap. His tunic was ripped open and he went into the mass with a slaughterhouse swing.

Matt Harrower was the first of the rebels to turn back, a man who liked to fight in the dark with the odds on his side. Drum leveled his revolver and picked him out of the saddle as he hit the road.

There was nothing now to keep the Bear Flaggers' courage from leaking away except a thing called *esprit de corps,* and the rebels had not been taught the meaning of that phrase. They broke. They tried to escape, and the men of the 4th California cut them down or took them prisoner. But when they started back up the cañon with the pay train in tow, only twenty men went with them as prisoners.

In the coolness of the late afternoon Drum dismissed the men on the drill field. They were tired and half sick with the things they had seen. But he liked the way they held their ranks until he released them. There was respect in it, for him and for themselves. Lieutenant Kelsey came to his tent after the surgeon had taken care of his wound. Kelsey looked sheepish.

"I don't believe we need to worry about the men any more, Captain," he said. "They've started wrangling about which platoon accounted for the most Bear Flaggers. I heard Corporal Foxen promise that his platoon would bag two men for the Second's one, next time they go out."

1st Sergeant McCullah was there, helping with the report. He said to Kelsey: "That's right, sir. They started gambling as soon as they got their pay. They're old soldiers, now." It was the first time McCullah had used the "sir" with Lieutenant Kelsey.

Passes were issued that night, and Drum rode into Belleville with Dave Rockaway. Just short of the town the Owen buggy came down the road in a swirl of dust, with Laurie on the seat. She stopped, Rockaway and Drum dismounting beside the buggy. They looked at her.

Laurie jumped down. She seemed completely oblivious of Rockaway. She took John Drum's hands and looked at him with relief and resentment. "The least you could do would be to let me know you were all right," she told him. "Your men have been coming in for an hour."

"I've been pretty busy," Drum said. "Of course, I wasn't sure whether it mattered much to you anyway."

Laurie did not seem to think it was funny. Then Dave Rockaway spoke.

"Hello, Laurie," he said. "I thought you'd be glad to know I was all right, too."

Laurie released Drum's hands. She said—"Oh. . . ."—and then stopped, without the words to go on.

Rockaway smiled. "I think maybe we went into this kind of sudden," he said. "Naturally I won't hold you to your promise, if you want to change your mind."

Drum watched the girl, enjoying her discomfiture. "I guess nobody's got to decide anything right now," he said. "Rockaway, suppose you ride down to the sawmill and see about that lumber."

Rockaway saluted. He said: "Yes, sir. Maybe I'd better scout around a little to be sure there aren't any more Bear Flaggers running loose, too. I know where I can get a guide."

"It might be a good idea," Drum told him.

He had dinner in the little room behind the shoe shop. Afterward, he and Laurie walked up the creek and sat on the bank to watch the sunset. Laurie was very quiet. It was plain that she had something deep and troubling on her mind.

"I've been thinking about us and the Army, John," she said at last. "I suppose I wouldn't mind being an Army wife so much, if that's what you want. After it's all over. . . ."

"After it's over," Drum interrupted her, "we're going back to Texas, Laurie. We're going to pry that ranch back out of the brasada and dare them to put us off. And I have a notion we'll still be there, twenty years from now."

Laurie did not ask what had changed his mind. Men made up their own minds, and women made the best of it. But it was in the smile deep in her eyes that sometimes a woman could turn her man's mind in just about the direction she wanted. . . .

★ ★ ★ ★ ★

THE DARK BORDER

★ ★ ★ ★ ★

I

The saloon was a dirt-floored layout with a tottering bar, homemade tables and chairs, and a scarred roulette wheel. The whiskey was bad but the golden Mexican beer was sweet and sparkling. There was a ruined piano but no girls—ruined or otherwise—and the big, rumpled, slightly seedy man called Hack Sherman had not been able to get this out of his mind.

"Three hundred miles from hell," he told Marsh Potter when they came in, "and no wimmen! It'll go hard with the ranchers' daughters hereabouts if I stay."

"We're not here for lollygaggin'," Marsh told him. "We'll either buy into this country or get out."

The question had been whether to join the rebel Mexican army marching on Chihuahua or to approach the thing differently by selling the army its beef. They had $3,000, enough for either venture. A couple of commissions, if they rode the revolution on in, would set them up as proprietors of vast *haciendas,* or whatever other favor they decided to ask. On the other hand, rebel scrip taken for their beef might be worth a lot someday. Or nothing. So they had come down here to the Big Bend, halfway to Chihuahua City, to see what might break.

They had been in the saloon less than two hours now, and what passed for a sizeable chunk of Texas cattle range lay in a heap of gold coin and yellowbacks between the knees of Hack Sherman and the big Texan he had tolled into a crap game. The man's name was Will Strayhorn, and at least three of the men in the saloon worked for him.

One of them, Frank Powell, his ramrod, kept saying in a pleading, shocked voice, his eyes worried under thorny brows: "Come on, boss! Miss Libby's going to be waiting for us. Miss Libby'd go straight up if she knew you were gambling with the ranch."

"Miss Libby will be the first lady preacher in the Big Bend one of these days," Will Strayhorn said. He had drunk more liquor than a man ought who intends to gamble heavily. This was one of Hack Sherman's talents. To get more whiskey into a prospect than he knew he was consuming. But Strayhorn had taken the bit in his teeth by demanding they start right out with a $50 ante!

Hack massaged the dice between his palms and blew on them. He was a large-shouldered, dark-skinned man of fifty with hair and sideburns as black as an Indian's. Riding his sorrel down the street like a grand marshal in a parade, he looked as though he might be going somewhere to sell snake oil or try a criminal case.

"Little Fever, babies!" he pleaded. "Uncle Hack wants to retire from this wicked gamblin' life!"

He let them strike the adobe wall and spin away, to simmer down with five spots. Little Fever.

Hack's guffaw rolled as he collected the winnings. Strayhorn looked stunned. A big man named Pete Brandon, wearing a black shirt, buckskin pants, and a Mexican sombrero, laid his hand on the rancher's shoulder. "*Bastante,* Will," he said. "Can't beat that kind of luck." He sauntered from the game to stand in the doorway, rolling a cigarette before he went on out.

Strayhorn wrote again in his tally book. He was a rude sort of man with an iron-gray beard and a red face. He had the manner of a cow country aristocrat. He handed the slip to Sherman. "This represents half my land and cattle. I've homesteaded the rest and can't put it up. This is my last bet. That much against your five thousand."

Hack looked at the paper in amusement. "Is this gent's paper any good?" he asked.

Everyone seemed a little shocked. Powell, the foreman, snapped: "Good as your gold. Boss," he pleaded, "you can make up the two thousand you've dropped, but you can't *never* make up them hundred thousand acres!"

Strayhorn kept his eyes on the swarthy man with the wide shoulders, black hair, and sinful face. Hack stood up. "Got to take this up with my pardner," he said.

He showed the paper to Marsh Potter, sitting at a nearby table. Marsh was as blond as Hack was dark. His face was deeply burned, and his hair was thick and tawny. He was a rugged young fellow who had broken horses, dealt cards, swung a sledge, and punched cattle. Of them all, he liked cowpunching best, but it paid the worst. A year and a half ago he had teamed up with this vain but likeable man who claimed to have done everything there was to do, and had the lines in his face to prove it.

Marsh's talent was to act as a governor on Sherman. Also he was skillful at getting them noticed when they hit a town. He rode a half-broken buckskin stallion with a black streak down its back, a *bayo-coyote*. The horse liked to pitch, and always got its chance when they rode down a main street for the first time. Marsh would let himself be thrown once, according to custom, and then come back to spur and fan the stallion till he was ready to quit. They had got into some interesting card games as a result of these exhibitions, some bronco contests, and a few brawls. In fact, it was what had brought them to the attention of this man, Strayhorn, who seemed dying for a game with out-of-towners.

Marsh handed the paper back. "Looks good to me."

Hack went back and knelt. Marsh drifted over. His heart was thumping; the profits of their whole come-what-may tour of Texas were in the pot, all but a few hundred dollars. They were perhaps one roll of the dice from being cattlemen or paupers, and Hack Sherman rolled a straight game.

Hack's large hands rubbed the dice. "Seven me, babies!" he pleaded. "Uncle Hack would shore look good behind a tally book!"

He rolled the dice, made them bounce hard off the wall, and snapped his fingers.

Will Strayhorn gazed a while at the dice, then stood up. "I'll draw you a map of the land," he said.

They went silently to the bar. Hack winked at Marsh Potter. Exultation was boiling in him, but he kept a decently sober face. Strayhorn said to the barkeeper: "One of my bottles, Mac."

He took it damned well, Marsh thought. Being drunk helped, but beyond that he did not grouse about bad luck but merely sketched a map on another tally sheet. The contours he sketched were familiar. They had performed an autopsy on this corner of the Big Bend before riding into Adobe. Strayhorn's land looked better than most. It was all so poor, such a tumbled red mud block sort of land, that only the mountain meadows, back from the Río Grande, boasted much grass. This whole southern loop of the Big Bend looked as though the devil had been through with a plow. The land had cracked open like the crust of a loaf of bread. Fantastic horns of rock rose above twisting rut-like cañons, high bluffs stood about, resembling the ruins of ancient civilizations.

Strayhorn gave the map to Hack Sherman. "Carmine Cliffs on the east," he said. "Río Grande on the west. Boundary between the places is Sand Creek. Horse Cañon is your southern boundary. By the way," he said, "does my loss entitle me to the dice as a souvenir?"

Hack laughed and fished them from a back pocket of his long frock coat. With his Colt, the gray-bearded cattleman smashed both on the bar. He looked into the gravel of powdered bone. He found no lead, no mercury, and smiled sardonically at the men. "My last hope," he said. He glanced at Powell. "Tell Libby I've gone on."

When the door swung, Marsh saw it was almost dark.

It was silent in the saloon. Pete Brandon had come back. He had a poncho thrown over one shoulder now. A well-built, swashbuckling man, he had a smile that was a white slash in his dark face. He poured liquor for the three of them from Strayhorn's bottle. "May you keep up your taxes better than Will did."

Marsh examined him while he drank the whiskey. Brandon was darkly good-looking, with an athletic body; the kind other men would envy, and women would invite despite their misgivings, for it was in his face that he would never love anyone the way he loved Pete Brandon.

"Pretty good piece of land?" Marsh asked.

Halfway to the door, Frank Powell turned back. He was a solidly made man of about forty, with the mouth of a hard-jawed bronco. "Best damned piece of land *you'll* ever have given to you!" He stalked out. In the street, Strayhorn could be heard swearing at his horse.

"Good?" Brandon smiled. "I'll give you six thousand for it right now."

Hack and Marsh looked at each other. Marsh shook his head. He had an idea land like that was worth keeping.

"I'm a shirt-tail neighbor of yours," Brandon said. "My land happens to be across the river . . . in Mexico. Good land, no taxes."

"No taxes?"

Brandon winked. "None that can't be straightened out. If

61

you're through here, I'll give you a line on the shortest way to reach the camp you'll call home. The home buildings are on Will's homestead section."

They walked a hundred yards north of the saloon. Adobe was a scrubby little crossroads town in the bottom of a wide, red-walled cañon watered by the Río Grande. The rancher pointed to a notch in the Carmine Cliffs, burning with the last light of the sun, by which they could steer. "About seven mile," he said.

They started back. "Will is one of those men that have to have the last shed whitewashed, while their cattle want for salt. He'll eat the best cuts of a steer and throw the rest to the hogs. He's back God knows how much on county taxes right now. You'll inherit part of 'em. It wasn't my fault he was in a corner. He'd had fifteen hundred dollars off me this year."

"Gambling?"

"Not exactly. . . ."

"You either gamble or you don't gamble," Hack declared.

"You don't always gamble in a saloon, though. Call me a speculator. I speculate that, if I take a herd of beef down to Chihuahua, I can sell it for twice what I'd get in Forth Worth. And I always do. But it's hard raising all the cattle I can handle, so now and then I bring a herd across the line. Oh, nothin' wet," he said. "They all carry vent brands. But the customs boys want too much. That's a spik for you. *Concusionarios* from the mangiest beggar right up to the *presidente*. They think I ought to pay ten *pesos* a head to bring the beef across! The hell with them! I square it with Will Strayhorn and bring my stuff across down below, at Horse Cañon."

His tone left the matter open; it put a little question mark beside it. Hack flipped a half dollar. "Well, we ain't temperance boys or nothing," he remarked.

"We are," Marsh cut in, "until we get around a little. Mention it again sometime," he told Pete Brandon. He did not mind hewing close to the line, but he would not be caught with half the line on his axe if he could help it.

As they reached the saloon, someone rode out of the dark grove of alamos behind the town. He was coming at a drumming lope, and hauled his pony around roughly as he reached the street. It was Powell. He saw Brandon and yelled: "Pete! Give me a hand with the wagon! Will's been throwed."

Brandon swore. "He must have been drunk to let that wrangler's special of his throw him! Why . . . why, hell!" he exclaimed. "Ain't that his roan right there at the rack?"

Powell swung down. "Damned if it ain't!"

Men were hurrying into the street. They began to check on their mounts to see whose horse the rancher had taken. But Marsh Potter already knew: he felt a little like a murderer. For he and Hack had driven Will Strayhorn to the wall, and the first thing Strayhorn had seen, when he left the saloon, was that cannonball Marsh called a horse, the buckskin named Comanche. He had seen the pitching exhibition in the street before the crap game and knew what the horse could do. Maybe it was just the devil-may-care act of a drunken cowman to take a horse he couldn't handle. Or perhaps it was the way a not-so-drunken cowman walked out of an intolerable situation.

II

Strayhorn's neck was broken. By the time they had brought him into town, the barber, who doubled as obstetrician, undertaker, and physician, arrived with flowing coattails. But the cattleman was dead. Libby Strayhorn, his daughter, had been found at the home of a friend. The body lay in the wagon. From the bench in front of the saloon, Marsh and Hack saw her standing there at the tail of the wagon.

In the unsteady light of a lantern, Marsh watched her through his cigarette smoke. Young, she appeared, slender and well-formed, wearing a dark basque and long skirt. Tragedy like this was something you could not get set for. You took it the way it was in you to take it, and Libby Strayhorn's grief was tight and suffocating. It meant to Marsh that she had had some practice in hard times. Maybe she had lost others close to her; maybe this high-living, high-handed father of hers had brought a bit of hard luck to those around him.

"Got no use for a jimber-jawed ox like that," said Hack. "Gamble with money he couldn't afford to lose, and then. . . ."

Across the street came Frank Powell. "She wants to talk to you."

Hack sent a coin spinning. "Heads I go, tails you go."

Marsh sighed. "I'll go."

Brandon was with the girl when he reached the wagon, standing with an arm about her shoulders. "Into each life . . . ," he was saying piously.

"Too much falls into some lives," Libby said wearily. Then she saw Marsh Potter standing with his hat in his hands, a big, unshaven young fellow wearing his guilt like a rope around his neck. She moved away from Brandon and stared at Marsh as though he were a strange animal captured and dragged into town. She said slowly, her voice low: "I just wanted to see what kind of man would do a thing like this. It's been a big night for you, hasn't it?"

It was the worse because her grief was quiet. He couldn't say—"Don't cry, lady."—pat her arm, and sneak away. She was looking right at him, and his shabbiness was on him like a dirty shirt. In his fancy Pendleton pants and expensive Stetson, he felt overdressed and underwashed.

"Miss," he said, "we hadn't no idea he'd do it. It was just a kind of a sudden game, and then. . . ."

"Do what?" she cried. "Are you implying that . . . that my father got that monster of yours *deliberately?* He'd been drinking. He didn't know his horse from anyone else's. You've got no right owning such a horse! A killer! If you hadn't. . . ."

It was unfair, but he made no defense. He knew that if her father had not been tolled into the game, it would never have happened. And she was such a frail little thing, pretty even with a red nose and swollen eyes, that he was touched. Yet she had plenty of spirit.

"It was nice of you to leave me enough land to raise some food on," she pursued him. "Is that customary with gamblers, after you've robbed a man?"

Marsh roused. "The game was straight, lady. Your father proved that by breakin' the dice afterward. And it was him that suggested playing for big stakes." Then he shook his head, glancing at her appealingly. "I don't want to argue with you, miss. I'm sorry we got him into the game. . . ."

"Then you admit you lured him into gambling with you? That's how you make your living, I suppose? Perhaps you'd teach me, now that I haven't enough land and cattle to. . . ."

Suddenly she leaned against the wagon and began to weep into her hands, the good, healthy kind of weeping that cleanses. Marsh was unable to resist reaching out and touching her shoulder. When she did not flinch, he patted her in rough sympathy. The contact acted electrically on him. It seemed indecent at this moment to think of her in that way, yet his mind was concerned less with her grief and more with noticing the trim femininity of her, the way her flesh was firmness under softness. Her hair was dark, braided, and worn low. There was a ring with a small ruby on the third finger of her hand, and Marsh's glance moved quickly to Pete Brandon.

"I'd like to make it up . . . some way . . . any way we can," he told her. She didn't answer, and Marsh cleared his throat, scratched his neck, and moved off across the street, toward his partner, Sherman.

"What did you tell her?" Hack demanded.

"Nothing. Said we wanted to make it up."

"Make it up," Sherman rasped. "How the hell you going to make up a thing like that? Besides, it wasn't our fault, no ways."

Marsh rolled himself a cigarette. "Let's sell back to her for five hundred dollars."

Hack gave a hard laugh. "Put five thousand on the block, and then sell the ranch for five hundred!"

Marsh didn't argue. But he sensed somehow that in five minutes a thin crack had opened in the ground between him and Sherman. He suspected faintly that theirs was a ruthless and rather selfish life, when it involved complications like this.

Powell had heard all this, but the sober, cynical ramrod had not removed his eyes from a point across the street. "I've been in just as tight spots with him before," Powell said slowly. "Today was one. He was gambling for tax money and something he owed for herd bulls. I guess you boys owe half those taxes, now. But Miss Libby owes for the bulls, and we haven't even got 'em any more."

Hack chuckled. "Looks like she could marry a certain well-heeled herd bull any time she wanted." He was watching the wedge-shaped Brandon beside the wagon.

"Marry that . . . !" Powell check-reined. "She's not that poor."

"Not to change the subject," Marsh said, "but what happened to the bulls?"

"You're not changing the subject. Six registered whitefaces, at two thousand apiece. We'd paid half. Rest will be due before long. But they're gone, every damn' one of them, the same place a few hundred other critters have gone."

"Where's that?"

"South!" Powell snapped. "Maybe them Mexican heifers have got something Texas cows ain't. A dash of Mexico City cologne under the armpits. Pete Brandon might know."

They bought a rusty spring wagon in the morning and loaded it with supplies. Driving east through the cottonwoods, they followed the tracks of Libby Strayhorn's wagon in the powdery dust. From Witch-Hazel Jones, barber, undertaker, and preacher, Marsh Potter had learned all about the funeral.

"Buryin' will be Sunday comin'," said Witch-Hazel. "That's five days. Buryin's are pretty big functions down here. Miss Libby's neighbors would take it a mite unkindly if she didn't give them time to drive over. Fish fries and funerals . . . about all that ever happens in the Big Bend. Pshaw, I wouldn't ride clean out there just to talk to myself, nohow! I've salted Will down slick with forty pounds of rock salt. See you there, boys."

About three miles out the road forked. It forded Sand Creek to approach Will Strayhorn's O-Six Ranch. They saw the buildings shining white on a bluff at the foot of the Carmine Cliffs. Their way was southeast. A score of dry streambeds slashed out from the base of the cliffs—a towering, rimrocked plateau dominating the jumbled lowlands. The graze was poor—sotol, lechuguilla, and burro grass. But there was sufficient water in earth tanks and thin streams worming along under leafy-headed cottonwoods.

It was six miles diagonally across their rough rectangle of lowland range to the line camp that would be their headquarters. It occupied a steep promontory above Horse Cañon, a deep furrow plowed from the base of the cliffs to the Río. The vista was masterful. Southward, beyond the cañon, it was over a shattered badlands where a goat could not have walked a mile without breaking a leg. No need to ask who owned that range. No one would have it. Westward, they could follow the twisting convolutions of Horse Cañon to the deep gorge of Mariscal Cañon, where the Río Grande was lost in silence and shadow.

But it was an eerie outlook. Like an eagle's nest, it made everything look distant and out-of-reach, emphasizing its loneliness. A man was on his own out here.

The camp was primitive. There was a small corral of ocotillo wands laced together with rawhide, a thorny enclosure a horse would not rub against twice. There was a mean hut of poles and mud, having no windows but some slots that closely resembled loopholes in a guardhouse. From a murky spring, water was carried in a rusted bucket a hundred yards. Stiff hides of beeves lay about, attesting that men ate well on this lost range, if nothing else. A wind blew steadily up out of the cañon, *hissing* through the toothed blades of a Spanish bayonet near their evening campfire.

Hack blew on his coffee and sighed. "That's a parcel of scenery for one roll of the bones."

"A lot of scenery," Marsh agreed, "but how many cattle? I didn't notice many on the way over."

Hack was unruffled. "The paper says half the cattle wearing the O-Six iron. If we don't see enough, we'll shove some across the line and start branding."

"We'll do it all according to the book," Marsh said. "There ought to be a range count. We'll split them up after. A Buzzard Slash would be a brand they couldn't squawk about. No chance of blotting an O-Six into a flock of straight lines."

"That might be a drawback in hard times." Hack chuckled. He saw Marsh's glance of inquiry, and sat back against a rock. "Well, we got to make some kind of count before anything else. Suppose we split up and kind of look things over? We'll get a rough idea, and then pick up a crew and go to work."

In the morning they spotted landmarks, chucked food into saddlebags, and set out. With an acute curiosity about Horse

Cañon, Marsh selected it for his starting point. A narrow cliff-side trail brought him down to the floor. It was like being in the bottom of a well. The walls went up steeply, and even at 9:00 little sunlight slanted over the rim to the damp, sandy floor. There were signs of a good many cattle moving down the cañon. He thought of Brandon's feeler: *I square it with Strayhorn and bring my stuff across at Horse Cañon.* And how many of Strayhorn's cattle did he move across with his own allegedly legal herds?

He kept thinking of this man Brandon, liking him less all the time, but only dimly aware of why it was. It all focused down on a tiny ruby on a girl's finger, the third finger of her left hand, and a proprietary arm placed across her shoulders by a double-talking dealer in wet cattle. Such thoughts were foolishness. He had been instrumental in the suicide of her father—he did not gloss over the bald fact of suicide—and how could he entertain the idea of being so much as recognized by her on the street? But Brandon . . . there was a man to capture a lady's heart, a big, grinning, saber-rattling sort who would buy you bonded bourbon and cut your throat so you couldn't drink it. But he wished he had half the rancher's polish and maybe he could square this business.

Then he got to thinking of those lost whiteface bulls of her father's, and the idea turned over and over until it acquired some polish. By grab, a man who brought back a prize like that would stack up with a girl! The first thing Marsh Potter knew, he was jogging along down the cañon, wondering how tough a crossing it would be and what he would find.

Horse Cañon joined the Río Grande at a wide and shallow spot in the river. It would be the only crossing for many miles. Elsewhere, above and below, the cañon wound and twisted through crumbled badlands. The country was an impressive ruin, hacked to pieces by erosion. Not far below, another cañon cut southwest into Pete Brandon's Mexican range. He crossed the river and followed it, looking for a trail to the higher land. Finally he discovered a cow trail mounting to a bony ridge. Looking about him, he realized the folly of starting such a hunt. A half million acres, perhaps, and he did not even know how long the cattle had been missing. Yet there was a well-grooved trail to follow, and it was for sure that wherever the bulls were, they would be cropping good grass, near water. Because he was also curious about the other cattle that had come this way so recently, he kept on.

It was wild and lonely country. He rode into the shank of the afternoon, along broken spines of rock, down nameless cañons, but always the not old trail of cattle went purposefully ahead, as if the cattle had been pushed. Near sundown, he broke into a small meadow in the foothills of a scrub-timbered range. It was a round meadow as shallow as a saucer, with a fair stand of grass. Cattle grazed here, but he saw no cowpunchers. After a moment he ventured farther. He kept moving through the herd, glancing at brands. Some Pothooks, Double Nines, a Panther Scratch, and a good sprinkling of Strayhorn's O-Six cows. So his ideas about Pete Brandon were not exaggerated. He could handle a knife and a handshake simultaneously.

Warily Marsh Potter inspected the environs of the meadow. No one in sight, and it was getting dark now and it seemed safe to camp here where there was water. But he risked no fire, and lay that night in a thicket with his head on his saddle. At dawn he rode on. The cattle trail split. He selected the one leading to high ground, knowing the graze would be best here. He had ridden about an hour when he topped out on a bench abutting against a flank of the mountains, watered by a small crystal stream and spotted with shaggy clumps of cedar. The bench was a couple of miles long but not far away; close to the slope of the hill was a camp. Three men sat around a breakfast fire.

Marsh kept his pony motionless while he looked about. A feeling of tension touched him. No one else in sight. Cattle grazing peacefully and some cows bawling about a stone corral where calves were penned for weaning. Good-looking stock, he thought. Not typical Mexican stuff, bone-racks with legs hanging down at the corners, critters with at least a foundation of Hereford. It did not take long for him to spot a couple of the bulls. They were built like boxcars, short-legged and broad-backed. No, Brandon was not selling animals like these to the Mexican army. He was starting a herd with them.

Potter dropped into the scrub brush at the edge of the bench and rode along. He found the rest of the bulls, two of them grazing, two in pens. At this end of the bench he was able to come into the open, release the two bulls, and start them along with the others, which he picked up as he rode. They were slow to drive, pampered, not built for rugged country. But he got them moving briskly back to the little gap where he had come up, and was almost over the rim with them when a shout rang out and a single shot echoed back from the hillsides.

He let them come. No use trying to outrun them with a cavalcade of aristocratic beef like this to push. But as the Mexicans loped in on their scrubby mountain ponies, he had his saddle gun across his lap. He raised one hand in greeting. *"¡Amigo!"*

Two of the men were thin-faced *vaqueros* with wispy chin beards, poorly clad in dirty shirts, leather pants that served also as chaps, and jipijapa straw sombreros. The other man wore a leather jacket in addition and had long, chiming Amozoc spurs at his heels. He was stocky, with the bleary-eyed, jaundiced look of the *pulque* devotee.

He gave Marsh a smile with a knife edge in it. *"¿A donde vas, compadre?"*

Marsh took from the sweat band of his Stetson the deed Will

Strayhorn had given him and Hack. "I've got a bill-of-sale for these *machos, hombre. Don* Pedro sold them to me in Adobe."

The Mexican took the paper and studied it. He was unable to read a word in Spanish or English, likely, but unwilling to admit it. "These no good," he declared. "Why don't you tell me before you take the bulls?"

One of the cowpunchers let his pony mince around behind Marsh, but he turned in the saddle and said quickly: "Where I can see you, Flaquito." The Mexican grinned and held his mount. Marsh said: "I didn't see any cause to get you off your hunkers. If you boys want to work so bad, you can help me drive these bulls to the river."

The *segundo* looked steadily at him out of his muddy, dark eyes. "The cattle are not going to the river, *compadre.*"

"Follow me and see," Marsh said. This was the moment of wire walking, and there was no certainty about what to do next. He was committed to a course of action that meant violence; there was no peaceful way to back out. But he turned his pony, the wild-hearted little Comanche who had killed a man out of sheer love of bucking, and made as if to follow the cattle. Yet in the instant when he heard the *creak* of leather, he spurred the buckskin forward and swung his rifle back with one hand. The move was lightning fast.

The *segundo* already had his fat cheek against the stock of a carbine. Marsh put a shot into the middle of his breast; it slapped him back against the cantle of his rawhide tree. He tugged at the loading lever as the pony began to pitch; the Mexicans could not get a shot at him. The *segundo* had fallen, but the remaining men had revolvers in their hands and one of them was lowering for a shot at the horse. Marsh hauled the pony up on its hind legs. He leveled the gun like a pointed finger; he saw the shot rip a bloody trench up the *vaquero*'s forearm and gouge his ribs. The man stared at his arm in shocked disbelief, and cried out as his horse, jumping from under him, spilled him on the ground.

With the temperament of a *prima donna*, Comanche began to squeal and fight again, so that Marsh had to grab leather. He had no time to eject the dead shell in his rifle. But when he shot an anxious look over toward the last of the trio, he saw him in unvaliant flight. When he could, he fired a couple of shots to help the man along, and rode at a lope down the trail from the bench.

III

The pressure did not leave until he had crossed the river. He blew out a long breath, and exultation began to fill him. He pushed the bulls along, whirling his rope, singing one of the sad songs cowboys loved:

> I'm an old cowpuncher,
> and here I'm dressed in rags;
> I used to be a tough one,
> and go on great big jags. . . .

And the whole thing, pushing some cattle along, watching the flash and crease of the water, seeing Comanche's ears flicking as he listened to the song, affected him deeply. He was halfway grateful to Hack Sherman. He had got him back into the work he belonged to, but as a *patrón* this time, not a ranni-han.

Suddenly it hit him. It was Saturday; the burying was set for tomorrow afternoon. Witch-Hazel Jones had let them know that the least anybody could do for Will Strayhorn was to be there at the burying. Well, Marsh Potter would be there, and with better than flowers: with six registered Hereford bulls.

He had to push them a little, but camped that night near a

muddy seep known as Chivas Well. Again he rode in the morning, collecting his lazy critters and hustling them along over his own broken range, across Sand Creek, and northeast toward the O-Six ranch buildings. It was past noon. Many wagon tires had cut the soft earth of the road, many pony hoofs. As he went through a motte of cottonwoods, he saw the throng near a bare patch not far from the big pole corrals. The ceremony had already begun. The preacher stood at the head of the dark slot in the earth, into which cowboys were already shoveling dirt.

Marsh hurried. The bulls smelled water, or cows, and began to ramble. They broke through a conclave of wagons. Alarm struck Marsh. The animals were heading fairly into the crowd around the grave!

He spurred ahead of them, swinging a coil of rope. *"Heah,* now, damn you! *Ha-a-a!"*

They swerved around him and came back onto the straight line. Witch-Hazel Jones spotted them. He was in the middle of his peroration: ". . . Ashes to ashes, dust to dust. In sure and certain hope of the resurrection into eternal life. . . ." He thrust one arm at the lumbering bulls and shouted. "Turn them critters aside, Potter!"

Potter, swearing and spurring, finally roped one of the animals. The crowd scattered like quail. He saw Libby Strayhorn picked up by Pete Brandon and carried behind a tree. His bull went down with a grunt and came onto his rump and forefeet, looking injured. Marsh and the bulls had the little family graveyard to themselves.

The whitefaces went on through and lunged down a crumbling bank to a creek. Marsh released the bull he had roped. People were coming back to the graveside, staring at him. Hack was there, Frank Powell, and now Libby, wearing a plain dark gown and with her rich, brown hair brushed smooth and parted.

She looked at him for an instant but said nothing. Brandon was beside her.

Marsh was aware of his own bright plaid shirt, horsehide vest, and conchoed chaps. At least he had his hat off, and he said numbly: "I found your bulls, Miss Libby. They . . . they got away from me."

"I know," she said. "Thank you. We haven't finished, you know."

Marsh faced the grave and bowed his head.

The burying ended tranquilly.

Afterward there was a cow-country feast. Plank tables under the trees accommodated the forty-odd mourners, about half of them relatives of the deceased. Barbecued beef and kid with plenty of come-back sauce steamed in great platters. There were pies and boiled spuds and buckets of coffee. Marsh had never seen anything like it. Pretty soon people were laughing and young bucks were pinching the girls. Strayhorn had had his hour; the rest of the day was for the quick.

But Libby, at the head of the table beside Pete Brandon, was as quiet as ever, eating little. Now and then Marsh Potter saw the ruby flash of the engagement ring on her left hand. Looking at the pious-faced scoundrel beside her, Marsh wanted to tear it off.

No one had much to say to Marsh, not even Hack who had a glint in his eye as he let him stew in his misery. Potter finished eating and walked over to his pony. He was tightening the mohair cinch when someone came up behind him. He turned to find Libby there, watching him. He hardly knew how to take her slow, grave smile.

"Don't feel badly about it," she said. "Frank went down to look at the bulls and he says they're ours, all right. And in wonderful condition. Where in the world . . . ?"

"Over a piece beyond Horse Cañon," he said. "They'd

bunched in a little meadow."

"I didn't know there were any meadows beyond the cañon. You mean you found them all together?"

"Don't know how it happened, but that was it."

"Well, it's wonderful, however it happened." She looked around. "We're going to have a talk about how to split up the cattle. Frank's waiting in the office now, with your partner."

They started for the big, flat-roofed Mexican ranch house. A porch spanned the front of it. Short *vigas* protruded from the whitewashed wall in lieu of eaves; grass and weeds tufted the roofline, where seeds had fallen on the earthen roof. Libby walked with a grace that made him feel clumsy. She was taller than the average woman, slender and well-formed.

"Powell told me about the game the other day," she remarked. "I didn't know about the tax money and the balance on the bulls. Those will be my big problems now. But I don't think I'll try gambling for them."

The tacit explanation pleased him. As they started up the steps, she put her left hand over his arm. He thought of that damned ring again, and glanced down at it. He frowned. It was gone. He saw it, then, on her right hand. She had moved it from the bespoken finger. . . .

The office was littered with mementos of the dead man: pipes and guns; Indian relics nailed to the walls; a half-smoked cigar in a saucer on the hand-carved cedar desk. Brandon sat in the chair at the desk, getting up quickly as Libby entered. Powell, the thorny-browed ramrod, sat on the wide mud window sill, while Hack Sherman, reflectively casting dice as he squatted on the floor, got up, rumpled and red-faced.

Powell had already got out the tally books. He was about to start negotiations when Marsh said ill-naturedly: "How does Brandon get in on this conference?"

Libby looked surprised. "Why, he's going to act as a sort of adviser until I get straightened out."

Brandon held a black *papel orozuz* cigarette lightly in his lips. Darkly good-looking, clean-cut if ruggedly made, he was the soul of integrity. But Marsh saw through the façade. It was like looking into someone's privy. He saw things about Brandon the man thought were secret, his treachery and baseness, his sterility of anything genuine. He was a Hack Sherman who had taken roots, without Hack's likeability. A roustabout and conniver, lacking the sense of humor to be anything but dog hungry for every dollar in sight. He thought with a start—*And where am I so different from either of them?*—and it made him like Brandon even less.

"Or maybe you'd like to be her adviser?" Brandon remarked.

"I'm not much for advising," Marsh said. "I may do some, though, before we're through. OK, let's go."

The tally books showed a total of about seven thousand cattle. "We'll make a better count than that when we start the beef cut in a couple of weeks," Powell said.

Hack flipped a coin and glanced at it, as though in his mind he had bet on the toss. "We'll settle for thirty-five hundred."

Libby frowned. "I suppose that would be according to the letter of the bargain. But we're sure to run under that number. Will you take half of what we find?"

Hack Sherman's large, lined face expressed displeasure. Marsh knew what he was going to say; he opened his mouth to object. Then he stopped and looked the situation over; Hack had as much say in it as he did, and technically, of course, he was right. So he kept still, hearing Hack say gruffly: "We'll split the difference. But not less than three thousand."

Libby glanced at Marsh as if she expected help from him. He looked away. She sounded a little irked. "All right, then. Powell will bring the crew over next week to start the roundup. Thank you for bringing the bulls back, Marsh. Thank you for nothing,

Mister Sherman."

Hack laughed. "Your daddy would have made out better if he'd had some of my ay-cumen," he told her.

"Probably he would. But I liked him about the way he was." She left the room. Powell nodded at the door and they walked out with a creak of boot leather and chiming *thud* of spurs.

Pete Brandon had brought along his range foreman. He was a lean, hook-nosed Mexican named Cayetano who had black hair and teeth stained reddish-brown. As they jogged along together on the road to Sand Creek, his face was somber. He looked like a *gringo*-hater; Marsh had about as much natural affection for him, and decided to get things started.

"You or this character responsible for those bulls?" he shot at Brandon.

Brandon's blunt face reacted swiftly, but Hack laid a hand on his shoulder, while looking at Marsh. "Son," he said to Potter, "you got to get those short hairs down. Any of our business how he runs his?"

"Yes," Potter snapped, "when he takes cattle we gambled for! I saw plenty of O-Sixes when I went after those bulls, and a steer ain't going to swim if he can help it."

Brandon shrugged. "Some may have got mixed in with my herds. Hack seems to think," he said, "that we could work out the same deal I had with the old man."

Marsh glanced quickly at Hack. "Sure. If you've got bills of sale on everything you bring across. I don't mean vent brands. I mean notarized pieces of paper."

"All right!" Brandon snapped. "But what about the herd I'm holding on Tornillo Creek right now? I've promised delivery on it next week. I've got to set out by Wednesday to make it. And I'm not going back to Alpine for bills of sale."

"No dice, then."

"Damn it, boy!" Hack exploded. "You can't raise cattle with

a Bible in one hand and a running iron in the other . . . not in this neck of the woods! Pete's going to do us a lot of good. He knows all them politicos."

"This beef-stealing ox never did anybody any good!" Marsh Potter said. "He had those bulls under a gun guard when I found them." He stared angrily at Hack.

Something crashed against the side of his head. He went down out of the saddle with a vacant ringing in his ears. He landed heavily and the jar both hurt and restored him. He lay on his side, looking up at the horsemen. He saw Hack yank the gun out of Pete Brandon's hand; Brandon had slugged him across the ear with the barrel of it.

He heard Hack snap: "When it comes to that, Pete, if you hit my pardner, you've hit me. Shuck down out of that saddle if you want a scrap. Marsh'll give it to you."

It seemed a watered-down sort of loyalty, but Marsh was glad enough to scramble up and wait for the rancher to dismount. Brandon slung his long body down, tossed his silver-heavy Stetson onto the ground, and advanced to meet him. He appeared less certain of himself. He was big and strong, but it remained to see how adept he was at rough-and-tumble.

Suddenly his arm stabbed and the fist hit Marsh in the middle of the face. His nose began to spurt. Tears brimmed. It was a fancy sort of punch and the kind Pete Brandon would love. Immediately the cowman tried to close in for the kill. Marsh took another blow on the ear in order to pull him into range. Then he piled onto him headlong, slugging, crowding him backward by sheer weight. He punctuated each swing with a grunted barroom curse. Brandon's spur caught and he sprawled.

Marsh jumped on him, knees searching for the cowman's belly. Brandon brought his feet up somehow and his sharp boot heels gouged the cowpuncher in the chest. It knocked the wind out of Marsh, hurt and disgusted him; he had been bested at his own game in the flurry. He landed on his back and had to crawl to get out of Brandon's way as he plunged after him. He heard Cayetano, the foreman, laugh. It shamed him: on his knees—crawling! He slewed around and got one foot under him, and he was still that way when Brandon swung savagely at his head.

Marsh ducked. Brandon did a fox-trot, trying to keep from falling as his weight followed his fist. Lurching up, Potter measured him an instant and fired a long shot into the side of his head. Cayetano stopped laughing. Brandon's swashbuckling grin was wiped out. He came around in a fumbling way. Marsh gave him the edge of his knuckles under the right eye. *He won't go courtin' with that eye!* he thought. Brandon was sweaty and bloodied. He tried to sway aside as Marsh drove for his jaw. He took a scraping blow that ripped the lobe of his ear.

Marsh gave a happy chuckle. He was dirty and fight-marked, but strong and hungry now. Brandon tried to carry the fight to him again by shoving in with both fists driving. Marsh took the blows on his body. He caught Brandon with a shoulder to the chin, then he chopped a right uppercut into his jaw. Brandon began to come apart, a glazed look in his eyes, his chin slack. Yet he still had the strength and sense to gasp: "Got enough, Marsh?"

Marsh said: "No spik English." He kept firing them into Brandon's high cheek-boned face until the face slipped away. He stood above Brandon a moment, feeling a triumph he knew could not last long. But while it lasted, it was sharp and intoxicating as whiskey. He was drunk on it when they rode off. It was all blended in with a ruby ring, and a farce that turned out not so badly as it had started.

IV

Out there in the eroded red wastes they pushed their two-man cow hunt for two days more. They learned some things about the country that hinted at short cuts, yet it was obvious that a full-scale roundup might take weeks. They had touched only the bottoms; back in the foothills and mountain meadows would be found most of the cattle. The work was exhausting. Marsh loved it, dust, brush scratches, and all, but Hack Sherman was past the age where he cared to break his neck busting wild cattle out of the breaks, and on Tuesday night as they dragged in he spoke his mind.

"You were a damned fool to whip Brandon. I told you he could do us some good. He was going to let us in on this deal of his for supplying cattle to the Maderistas. He'd take anything we wanted to send down for only twenty-five percent of what they paid at Chihuahua City."

Marsh dropped his saddle just inside the mud hut. "We'd still have to ranch to have anything to send, wouldn't we? And we could take them ourselves."

Hack slung a piñon branch into the cook hole and bent to light a fire. "We could buy herds like Pete does," he said. "Just act as commission merchants, like. I reckon if we was to ride up to Tornillo Creek, where this herd of Pete's is, and tell him it was jake all around, we could still cut in with him."

Marsh Potter's glance was cool. "Sometimes I think you're two men, Hack. One of you has a heart as big as a washtub. He doesn't take himself too seriously, but he knows what's going on. The other man's got an eye as cold as a church deacon's smile. He'd sell a drunken cowman and his daughter down the river to win a ranch he doesn't want. Maybe he'd sell his own pardner out, how do I know? But I do know we aren't going to peddle stolen beef for Pete Brandon or anybody else."

Hack sat there on his hunkers for a while, slicing onions into a Dutch oven, the whole thing turning like smoke fumes in his mind. Then he wiped his knife on the seat of his pants and grinned.

"I never did like church deacons," he said, "so I guess I'll be the other jasper. Toss me them spuds, will you, Marsh?"

They had one of their old-time palavers over a quart of whiskey that night. Restored by coffee, food, and whiskey, Hack Sherman was himself. He was the likeable windbag who wore a brass medallion on a silver chain around his neck, nestling in the thick black chest hairs, a medallion on which was stamped: *GOOD FOR ONE BEER. BUCKHORN BAR.* The Hack Sherman with half his left ear missing, which he liked to explain he had lost in an Indian fight. "I was in the teepee with his squaw when the Indian come in."

It was almost like old times, but something wasn't quite right. It was not that Hack had changed, but that Marsh had. He had been a boy too long, but now he was beginning to grow up. A lot of it was that he was in love with Libby Strayhorn, no doubt about that. The hand-stands he did so well did not seem to impress her. But partly it was that he had remained in mental knickerbockers until he was about to burst out of them. He was coming of age spiritually. He almost wished he could remain a boy. It was more fun.

In the morning, Hack paid for his debauch of the night before. He hunched, groaning, on his sougans. "Gettin' old, Marsh! Can't take likker and onions together no more. Got a bellyache fit to draw a man's knees up to his chin. Just bring me some coffee, would you, boy? . . . and that Perry Davis Pain Killer out of my war sack."

Marsh fixed him up. Unshaven, unwashed, with dark loops under his eyes, Hack looked sick enough for two men. "Sure you're all right?"

"Shore. You go on when you're ready. I'll be along directly."

Marsh saddled and stood on the rim of the cañon, looking out over the badlands to the south, with the wine of sunrise spilling over them. It was too fine a morning to be sick. The mockingbirds were warbling like fools; the jays screeched at him to get out of camp so they could get to their pillaging. The air was still cool, filtered by night mists. He knew how the Mormons must have felt when they said: this is the place.

He swung past the mud hut on his way out. Hack waved at him. "Say, did you notice that big chimney rock above Goat Wash?" he called. "Seen a lot of tracks heading around it. Maybe a spring up yonder, or a lick or something. Might be a lot of them up there."

"I'll take a look."

Potter reached the point in about an hour. It was in the foothills near the cliffs, a jungle of sotol and maguey, the terrain dry and rocky. He saw no cow tracks, but identified the chimney rock. He rode around it and discovered a few horse tracks. Hack's, probably. He rode on up the wash. The tracks separated into two distinct sets. Then one of them mounted the right bank and the other climbed the left. It was odd, because both horses had been going in the same direction. They could not have been Hack's coming and going tracks.

His reasoning was at this point when a scrape of sound made him look about. But it was too late for him to avoid the rope that settled about his shoulders. A horseman sat his pony in the fortress of stones above the wash. It was Cayetano, Brandon's foreman, who came spurring down the sandy bank with the other end of the rawhide reata lashed about his saddle horn.

Marsh was plucked neatly out of the saddle and hurled to the sand. He began to struggle, but instantly the rope snapped tight and dragged him over the bottom of the wash. Sand burned and blinded him; small stones struck his shoulders, his head, his hip bones, wracking him. He rolled and slid and bounded. He was scared and confused, helpless as a pullet in the bottom of a sack, and, if he knew one thing, it was that when they shook the rope loose there would be nothing left of Marsh Potter but the rags of a fine shirt and pair of britches.

Then the lurching stopped. He lay flat on his face on the bed of the wash. A hand turned him roughly. Pete Brandon's face was a blurred picture of satisfaction.

"Got to be hard for this country, Marsh," he said. "Talkin' hard ain't enough. There's no stage out of here, but you got a good hoss. This is so's you won't forget, and come back."

His shoulder rolled; a coil of hard rawhide rope *hissed*. It struck Marsh in the face. He groaned and found the strength to cross his arms over it. The rope *hissed* again; his chest was lacerated by the hard strands. It went on for half a dozen strokes, and then Cayetano rolled him over and they were giving his back the treatment when he lost consciousness.

He stayed at the spot until the middle of the afternoon. For a while he became sick every time he stood up, but at length he made it to a spring and soaked his head, scooped water over his shirt, and lay on the damp sand, feeling every welt on his head and body.

When he could feel anything beyond pain, it was rage. Not rage with Hack Sherman. His treachery was stunning as a thunderbolt, but the rage was not for him. It was for himself, for being so poor a judge of men that he mistook lead for gold. He'd been living with a liar the last year and a half and thought the man just a good-natured clown. Now he knew that when they had occasionally talked seriously, when he unashamedly disclosed fragments of boyish ideals, Hack, soberly agreeing, was thinking: *You danged young greenhorn. Fine talk for a man.* And Hack must have known that their friendship would someday end in this fashion. The lion and the lamb lay down together only in the Good Book.

There was rage in him for these things, and it made him want to kill. A blind need to purge himself of this hatred shook him. That was when the rage veered into its proper channel.

About 3:00, with the sun in Mexico, he pulled himself into the saddle. He let the horse take him back to within a quarter mile of the camp, dismounted, then walked on in. He carried his rifle, stepping quietly up the trail. Hack's horse saw him but did not whicker. Hack was in the mud hut.

When he heard Marsh, he whirled from the table where he was stuffing articles into his old canvas bag. After an instant's staring, he swore.

"Great God! What cliff did you fall off of?"

Marsh let his thumb rub the slick walnut gunstock. There was hardly an inch of skin left on his face. Bloody scabs took the place of skin. His shirt was gone, his undershirt bloody and torn. He brought the gun up, and Hack's hands reached back to grip the edge of the table.

"What is it? I don't git this!"

"Yes, you do. Right in the wishbone."

"Why, boy! You didn't think I had any. . . ." He blundered to a stop.

"Any part in it? Shore did, Hack. You thought you saw some cow tracks up there, did you? Wrong. They were badger tracks. And I walked right into the hole. But I came out alive, and I still haven't got the sense to quit."

Hack was thinking of the little double-barreled belly gun he carried in an inner pocket of his coat. His eyes told Marsh that. He said: "Take off your coat." Hack shucked out of it carefully. But now his face was less concerned with his position, for he knew he was not going to be killed.

"That's right," Marsh said wearily. "I haven't the guts for it. Like you, Hack, only I haven't even got the guts to let somebody else do it for me. Get out the money and split it."

There was still the $5,000 they had taken from the saloon in Adobe. Hack made two equal piles of it. His manner was a little disdainful as he finished and looked across the table.

"I've got an idea anything that belonged to you might bring a man bad luck," Marsh said. "Take it and get out, you brass-plated Buffalo Bill."

Sherman deposited the money in his bag, shook the Derringer from his coat onto the floor, and pulled the coat on again. "What you going to do, Marsh?"

"Ranch. I'll pay back your half when things are cleared up. Send me your address. But don't ever come back."

Big Hack Sherman strolled from the mud hut, saddled and packed, and casually rolled and lighted a cigarette. He swung into the saddle. "*Adiós*, kid. Good luck." Just before he reached the turn, he twisted to shout: "I never did tell you about that crap game, did I? The dice Strayhorn broke were one of my square sets. I used tappers on him. Handier'n hell! Just tap them right and you can roll any combination you can think up!"

V

The snapper. Let a man think he had slept with a leper without catching anything, and then point out that unfortunately there was nothing left of his face. He had been all ready to make his stand. When it was over, he would have ridden across Sand Creek once more to claim his bride. The dragon killer of the Big Bend, the Texas Lochinvar. He was still going back there, but with a different story to tell now.

God, if Strayhorn hadn't got Comanche! He drove his fist against the rough hut wall. The one thing he could not fix up. He could bring back six bulls from hell. He could lick Pete Brandon, and, if necessary, he could kill him. But he could not bring a man back from the grave.

That night he slept in the brush. He hoped they would come, any or all of them. They did not. In the ruddy dawn he gazed down into Horse Cañon. All cool and quiet down there, but one day soon a herd would come down the cañon. He would have liked to be here when they came, but it was no fight of his. It was Libby's, and Frank Powell's, and her cowpunchers, if they would make the fight.

He packed what food he could carry and set out, leaving the wagon. It was well past noon when he arrived at the O-Six. The corral was full of cow ponies, saddles lined the top rail. Powell had brought his men in from the isolated line camps of the ranch for the start of the roundup. The ramrod saw him as he left his horse to start for the ranch house. Marsh had donned his extra shirt, but it did little for him.

Powell's crisp gray eyes pinched. "I heard you and Brandon tangled," he grunted. "I see now it was you and a buzz saw."

"We tangled twice," said Marsh. "I've got something to tell the boss."

Powell nodded at the house. "She'll be out. You fellers ready for the roundup?"

"There won't be any. Sherman lit out last night. I'm on my way now."

He saw Libby come onto the long porch. He walked on, to stand at the bottom of the steps, looking up at her; she was fresh and trim in a white shirtwaist and dark skirt. Suddenly he did not know whether he was man enough to tell her the truth. It would be easier to let her think he was plain big-hearted, or even that he had been scared out. Then she was coming down the steps to him. She stood a step above him with her hands just touching his face. Women were queer creatures, he thought. He'd be hung for a horse thief if she weren't crying.

"Oh, Marsh. Marsh," she said.

"Ain't you ever seen a skinned mule before?" Marsh said. "I fell off a cliff with Pete Brandon. You weren't in love with that . . . with Pete, were you?"

She was still looking at him. She did not seem to hear him. "We'll have to do something for those scratches. Come inside." Halfway up the steps she glanced at him. "In love . . . with Pete? Why, he's nothing but a human pouter pigeon! Eternally running around like a Mexican dandy. What made you think I was?"

"I just wanted to be sure before I told you something. I found those bulls on his land. I guess you know what that means."

"I know. We found his brand on them later."

Marsh had not even looked at the brands. They went into the cool dusk of the big ranch house. But suddenly, as he realized what he was doing, he retreated to the door. "Forget the scratches, Libby. I've got to tell you something. I'm on my way out. The ranch is all yours."

She sat on a rawhide chair, her hands limply in her lap. "Just like that? I don't have to buy it or anything? Surely Hack didn't agree to that?"

"We worked out a deal. He's already left. We had a little argument over it. He told me . . . something I didn't know, and it kind of changed things."

She looked steadily at him. "What happened between you?"

The bitterness entered his voice. "Hack turned me over to Pete and that walleyed ramrod of his. They drug me down a wash and then licked the. . . . So I went back to the mud hut and we broke it off."

"I knew you'd have to break with him, sooner or later," she said softly. "He wasn't your kind. You're honest and clean. Not Hack Sherman."

Honest and clean. Laughter rang in his head. He reached back and his hand found the screen door.

"I was feeling *muy hombre* when I started over here," he said. "Now, I guess the best I can do is the same as Hack did. Spill it an' git. Libby, the dice we licked your daddy with were loaded. I didn't know it till Hack told me. I thought it was square. So it's all O-Six again. There never was a Buzzard Ranch. I wish I could bring him back, too, but this is the best I can do. *Adiós, chata.*"

He got halfway down the steps. She ran out onto the porch. "Marsh, you come back here!" He let himself be half pulled back into the house. Libby held him by the arms. "You are a simple one, aren't you? Everyone but you simply assumed the dice were loaded. Couldn't you tell by looking at him?"

She seemed to miss the point entirely. He shook his head. "I guess I never looked at him. I liked the big horse thief. I liked his windies and the way he'd laugh when we lost. I didn't know he was that low." It was hard talking through the dryness in his throat. "But how do you know I wasn't in it with him?"

Libby was cool and imperative as a candle flame in the gloom, graceful and slender, impossible to lie to even if a man wanted to. "You weren't in it with him, were you?"

Marsh suddenly wanted to laugh. He could feel his face cracking when he grinned. "I was as big a dupe as Will, but I happened to be on the right side. That's how it was, and it's how come I'm leaving. Maybe you didn't know Brandon's bringing a herd down Horse Cañon pretty soon. I'd let him be, if I were you, but I'd move all my cattle away from that end of the ranch and keep plenty of line riders over there."

"You mean you'd leave me to fight this out . . . alone?" she demanded.

His heart gave a bound. "I can be had, ma'am, for thirty a month. I've had experience punching cattle, not to mention Pete Brandon."

"I'm hiring you as range foreman," she said quickly. "Brandon will be just one of your jobs. The main one will be to prove that you can be steady as well as footloose. I've had enough of gambling men and high livers. You can stay here as long as you apply yourself."

"I'll be the applyin'est range foreman you ever had," Marsh told her. "But right now I'm going to apply myself to Brandon. Can I take a few boys along for company?"

"Take them all. But, Marsh. . . ." Her hands held the edges of his vest. She regarded him earnestly a moment, but ended by shaking her head in vexation. "No use telling you not to be foolhardy. That's all you know how to be. Only, try to come back in better shape this time, will you?"

VI

The O-Six crew was an assortment of Mexican and American cowpunchers, one as dark as the other and all of them as deeply burned as the Texas earth. Their clothing was bull-hide and denim armor, fashioned to stand the slash of catclaw and mesquite thorn; they themselves were hard, unimaginative men who seemed to have grown out of the soil. Many of them wore ponchos, apron-like *armitas* instead of chaps, and sombreros shaped like conical sugar *piloncillos*. A lean old bronco stomper called Rojo—Spanish for Red because of his wattle-like skin rather than his hair—listened as Marsh talked to Frank Powell. He seemed to be spokesman for the rest of the crew, and Marsh got the idea that, if he didn't like what he heard, none of them would go. They squatted on their heels before the bunkhouse, smoking.

"All I'll promise you," Marsh told them, "is that Brandon is a cow-stealing border-jumper, and that he ain't going to be a cow thief any more after I get finished with him. He's coming through that cañon *poco tiempo*, and I'm going to be waiting for him, whether you go with me or not."

Powell's eyes shucked through irrelevancies and looked right at a man. "Who says you ain't his bellwether? You were *muy amigo* with him last time I was with you two."

"You missed a couple of our hand holdin's. I licked him, and then he and that hook-nosed Cayetano licked me. But I bet I win two out of three."

Rojo scratched his skinny neck, peering in morbid fascination at Marsh's face. "Ah reckon he didn't scratch hisself up that way, Frank. Ah know Ah wouldn't."

Marsh had told them all about his breakup with Hack Sherman. In no mood to beg favors, he stood up. "Well, that's the story. You can do what you damned well please. But I'm going back over there tonight."

He heard them discussing it as he walked over to the corral. He gave the latigo a tug. Without waiting for them, he mounted and rode off. The sun was deep; it would be long after dark when he reached the cañon. Even then it might be too late. Or they might come by night, and he would have a hell of a time picking out Brandon in the dark, for he couldn't stop all of them.

He had gone about a mile when he heard them behind him, streaming down through the gap at Sand Creek, loping up over a bald red ridge to catch him and ease their horses into a trot. There were a dozen of them. Powell had left the rest at the ranch. "Well, I guess we'll have a crack at it," he said.

Night caught them at Chivas Well. They watered the horses sparingly and threaded on through the gullies. It was close to midnight when they straggled into camp above Horse Cañon. The horses were about beaten. They made such a turmoil with their blowing, rolling, and snorting that it was hard to tell whether anything was going on in the cañon or not. Marsh stood close to the edge of the cliff, which descended in great rimrock leaps to the bottom; he noticed that Powell judiciously stood behind him. The river flowed below, dark and silent, stippled with light from a splinter of moon, but the cañon was deserted.

"We'll have to go down to find out whether they've already been through," Marsh declared. "Better go afoot. Leave a couple of boys with the horses. Catamounts might bother them."

He had to watch his footing on the ledges. It was an almost straight fall to the bottom. The huge blocks of stone were water-streaked, tufted with coarse grass and infrequent yucca. He reached the floor of the cañon, a damp alley of rock and sand. The stream was a fifteen-foot path of water between hedges of the wolf willow. Marsh examined the sand. The hoof prints were old ones. He looked around at Powell.

"This as good a spot as any?"

Powell sent a glance around the dark walls. "Not much cover," he said. "But then there ain't much cover anywheres, in this grave-digger's nightmare."

"Let's wait for daylight. If they don't come then, we'll get some grub from the mud hut and dig in."

In the darkness, the ten of them stirred around until they had found what would pass for redoubts. The rubble at the base of the cliffs was small. Marsh, crossing the small stream, wedged himself in between two rocks, laid shells on one, and laid his saddle gun across the parapet.

After hours they heard a sound, a series of light footfalls. A mule deer came down the stream, pausing near Marsh to nuzzle the quiet water and drink. Suddenly it threw its head high, looked about, and whirled to race up the cañon with its swift, awkward leaps.

Nice, thought Marsh, *if the cattle pulled one like that!* But cattle were not apt to take alarm unless they spotted a man. A man afoot would scare them where a rider could sometimes pass through a herd without disturbance.

Then a second interval stretched away, broken at last by the tumble of a small rock down the cliff. Marsh's nerves pounded. But no other sounds followed. He heard someone cough. A cowpuncher said: "How 'bout a smoke, Frank?"

Powell said tersely: "Chaw it."

That got Marsh to needing a smoke. He rolled a cigarette and sucked on it but did not light it. *If I do much of this,* he thought, *I'd better carry a plug of Navy.* And he thought about Libby, and how right everything was going to be when it was all over and behind. By looking at future pleasures, he could forget that right now he was nervous as a cat. The cigarette was no consolation. He emptied the paper and tucked the dry flakes under his lower lip. That was worse, and he was still spitting when Powell said: "She's gittin' light."

Overhead, light burned on the rimrocks and the dark sky was shot with veins of gray. But little light came down to them. Gradually the sky lightened, until a murky daylight existed in the cañon and he could see the others in their spots. Most of them had cold cigarettes in their lips.

"Somebody ought to git some coffee an' crackers down to us," Rojo complained.

Marsh stood up and stretched. "I'll make some and bring it down. You don't mind all drinkin' out of the same tomato can, do you?"

He jumped the stream and started up the trail. Weariness sanded his eyes and slowed his movements. About halfway to the top he paused to look down. A couple of steers ambled into view up the cañon. Several more followed them. They were so unhurried, it was all such a natural thing to observe the cattle trailing along, that he merely stared at them for a moment. Then it got through to him. He opened his mouth to yell; he raised his gun to fire a warning shot. He did neither, but tossed a rock over side and started down the trail.

He was still fifty feet above the floor when the cattle started past. The leader was an old longhorn walking with head up, vigilant. Behind him came other long-legged critters, and then the main body of the herd, largely Hereford. They were walking easily in loose file, not being hurried evidently. Marsh stood on the trail, afraid to go on down. He could see the men below, none of them well hidden. But for ten minutes none of the cattle spotted a cowpuncher, until suddenly an old, often-branded mossyhorn shied, threw its head up, and tried to turn back. The unreasoning panic instinct of the cattle flared. There was a jam in the cañon, some of the cows trying to push on, a whole log jam of them attempting to turn back.

Marsh cursed. The men in back would know something was going on and be on the alert as soon as they sensed the difference in the herd. He ran on down the trail. There couldn't be many more cattle, he thought. The riders must not be far up-cañon.

He shouted at the others and started up. Rocks piled along the base of the cliffs kept the cattle from filling the whole cañon. But it was rough passage over them in boots. About a hundred yards up, the cattle were still coming along, screened from the milling column below by a turn. They began to react violently when they saw the cowpunchers at each side of them; Marsh now had no hope of surprising Brandon and his crew.

He heard a man bark a shrill cowboy yell. It came from beyond a bend. The cattle were hustling past it. Marsh raised his arm and picked a spot. Rojo, across the cañon, went to one knee beside a rock and threw his shell belt across it. The first of the *vaqueros* came in sight—a slim Mexican with a mustache like strands of frayed silk cord. He was chousing the steers along, the knees of his pony booting an old bull in the rump. A couple of other men came in view, one of them an American with his Stetson hanging by its lanyard. Other men came in sight, taking it easy but beginning to show some curiosity about the behavior of the herd.

At last Marsh saw the face he had been looking for—Pete Brandon's. Brandon rode with two other men. One of them was Cayetano. The other was a big, frock-coated man wearing yellow boots. Hack Sherman.

A shot splintered the dull thunder of hoofs. The lead cowboy lurched in the saddle. Rojo, with no false pride about giving warning, had fired first. Instantly the whole scene was agitated into violence. There were a dozen odd men with Brandon, all of whom were suddenly doing something noisy or unpredictable. Horses and cattle milled; men slid out of their saddles or stuck to them as if safety lay nowhere else. But Brandon and the other pair curbed their horses and tried to see exactly what the caper was all about.

Shots began to fill the cañon with thunderclaps. It seemed that the racket must shake the stones loose. It drummed against the ears and eyeballs; the flashes were swift flame stripes across the weak daylight. Cayetano was a little ahead of Brandon, a natural target. Marsh was as steady as a rock, needing no rest for his gun barrel as he balanced his sights and pressed the trigger. Cause and effect were simultaneous. The hook-nosed foreman clasped his shirt front in his fist and looked back at Brandon as if to say something. When his horse pitched, he was thrown. He lay there on the sand, a ragged blood splotch on the back of his jacket showing where the bullet had emerged.

Marsh walked forward another dozen feet as he pumped a fresh shell into the breech. Brandon's spurring about failed to rally the bunch. Four or five men were down or sitting shocked in their saddles. It was bad for the morale of the others. Two of them turned to race back up the cañon. Brandon shouted at them; his face darkened and he fired at one of them with his

Colt, and dropped the man as he rushed by.

Powell knelt beside Marsh. He put a hard cheek against the stock and a few seconds later the gun kicked and rocked his shoulder. Pete Brandon fell across the swell of his saddle, the huge Mexican horn thrusting into his groin. Powell fired once more and for Brandon it was over.

"The times I've wanted to do that," Powell muttered.

It was a rout, after that. Some of the *vaqueros* made it down the cañon through the press of cattle. A couple rode upstream, one of them being Hack Sherman. Marsh rushed his shot, missed Hack but saw his horse falter. It lunged to its forelegs, throwing Sherman to the ground. He got up in a stumbling crawl and disappeared around the bend. His hat lay on the sand.

Marsh followed, determined to see the end of this. He walked past the bodies of Brandon and Cayetano, through the wounded who lay in the cañon. He knew his big, four-flushing ex-partner would not run far. He walked along with the carbine ready to snap against his shoulder. He passed a couple of bends without seeing him, but when he walked around the third, he saw a dark form lying among the rocks on his left, fifty feet ahead.

Hack fired first. The shot caught the flare of Marsh's batwing chaps and wailed off a rock behind him. What was good enough for Hack was good enough for him. He went down on the sand and took an infantryman's stance. He heard Hack call in a breathless voice: "Don't do it, boy! Not to your old pardner! There's still a million towns waitin' for us, boy, a million poker games. . . ."

No, Marsh thought, *not even one game.* But it hurt to send the shot away; there was a certain magnificence in Hack's depravity. He felt the jolt of the carbine and saw him start, his legs slowly drawing up. He got up slowly, with an eye for treachery, but after a moment, not wanting to look long, he went back down the cañon.

Marsh helped them with what had to be done, but none of it touched him. He was far away, living days that were yet to come. He let the tranquility of those dreams blunt the ragged edge of his emotions. Up there with Hack Sherman lay another man, one no one else would notice when they buried the gambler. It was the ghost of Marsh Potter, and it wanted burying badly, for there was no one to claim it. Everything Marsh wanted now was tied up with things he would have laughed at a month ago—hard work, peace, and the quiet love of a girl who meant all these things to him.

★ ★ ★ ★ ★

CHIVAREE

★ ★ ★ ★ ★

In the dark cabin Jim felt Nettie's body start and turn toward him. Her Indian blood, he reckoned—rousing on a sound no louder than the whicker of a horse. He held her tightly with one arm while he groped beside the bed for his rifle.

"Stay right here, Nettie," he whispered. "Keep the blankets about you."

"Jim . . . Jim," she whispered. "What is it?" She had seen his bare arm hunting the rifle.

"Don't know," Jim Croft grunted, piling out into his boots and heaping the blankets on her. There was no telling what—but blankets would sometimes turn a bullet.

In his nightgown—which Nettie had made him and he had to wear—he slipped to the window. He had hardly reached it when the gunfire let loose again. The bullets came in a slogging rhythm against the mud wall under the eaves. It was a shattering thing, but Jim understood, now, and was reassured.

He let the bullets run out, then he called to his wife: "Chivaree! Dress quick and rustle all the cups you can."

There was a blood-chilling sound, ripped through with a wild coyote yelling. There was some grunting, too—all the sounds that passed for Indian. He wondered if Nettie got it. If she didn't get it, Reuben Lightfoot—and the crowd he had brought along for the fun—would make it plain enough.

Again the guns blasted at the cabin; hoofs *thudded* in the corral, and the chickens were squawking. Nettie came to him, pressing fearfully against his side. Her dark hair hung in two long braids over her shoulders. Her breast was soft against his arm, and Jim wanted poignantly to make it all smooth and easy for her, to keep her pride as shining as her eyes.

"What will they do, Jim?"

"Just horse around a bit. Don't let on you're scairt. But don't take anything from Rube Lightfoot, either. The others will be all right, unless. . . ."

He watched her pull her flowered calico gown down over her nightdress. This dark-eyed wife of his—he loved her so much it was hard to bear. Nights, he couldn't squeeze her close enough; days, he'd make chores to take him back to the cabin. They were singing-happy, but inside they had both been waiting for the thing that would determine whether they would be neighbors or outlanders—whether a squawman and his half-breed wife would be accepted in this recently Indian country. And now Rube Lightfoot had brought it to them.

Jim opened the door. "When you lobos get done howling at the moon, come in and wet your whistles!" he shouted.

The gobbling and firing ended. Lightfoot's rain barrel bass rumbled. "Well, she ain't scalped him yit, evidently!"

Out of the sagebrush tromped a dozen men. Boots scuffing, smelling of man sweat and horse sweat, unshaven and brazen-eyed, they crowded into the cabin. On the table, Nettie Croft had placed a jug of corn whiskey and all the vessels that could pass for cups, including two small pottery pans.

"Missus Croft," Lightfoot said, "you set a mighty fine table." He took one of the pottery vessels.

The other men crowded in to the whiskey, cowpunchers who worked for Reuben Lightfoot and small ranchers like Jim. Lightfoot said, tossing a hand at the rumpled cot: "I see as you folks were in bed."

"Where else, at two o'clock in the morning?"

Nettie flushed. Jim's smile was varnish over the rough timber of his dislike. Lightfoot was a huge turkey buzzard of a man, belligerent and bungling. He had got rich merely by getting onto this range first. It took more cleverness, now, but one day the likes of Lightfoot would be made to prove up on some of the range they claimed.

Lightfoot had a lofty nose and an oval-shaped black chin-beard. He inspected Nettie with a savoring curiosity. "I'm Rube Lightfoot, Missus Croft. I expect you've heard of me."

"I have, Mister Lightfoot. You're quite famous."

Lightfort rubbed whiskey from his chin. "Some of your people were quite famous, too, ma'am. I hope none of your lodge was at Little Rosebud. I lost a brother there."

"Those were Sioux, Mister Lightfoot. My mother's people were Cherokee. My father, you know, was a Scot trader."

Jim shoved between them. "Boys, you aren't drinking." He refilled Lightfoot's cup and started around. Suddenly he heard Nettie cry out; he whirled, the jug lying across the crook of his arm. Dave Banta had picked her up by the waist and was holding her so that her dark, brushed hair was against the herringbone rip-rapping of the ceiling. A tall, skinny man in overalls, Banta had eyebrows and mustaches as yellow as chick fuzz.

"Always heard you couldn't creep up on an Injun!" he said. "Dang' lie!"

The men in the cabin, Jim thought, would gag on their laughter. They slapped their legs and hooted, and tall John Porter howled and slapped his palm against his mouth, making the gobbling cry they had heard from the darkness.

Jim stood with a grin pasted on his face, despising them.

Banta set the girl down. She smoothed her dress over her hips.

"Of course, I'm only half Indian, or I'd've heard you coming," she said. Then: "I could make coffee and biscuits."

"Never mind," said Lightfoot. "I only come over on business anyhow. Directly we'll go along."

"Business?" asked Jim. "With me?"

"Two things, Croft," Lightfoot said. "You're overworking that Tres Piedras pasture of mine. You figuring to set up a Cherokee village for those papooses you'll be getting soon? I moved your stuff off it today."

"My deed says it's mine. I'll move them back tomorrow."

Lightfoot smiled, and a hard light came into his eyes. "It ain't the place of a guest to contend with his host. We'll talk about it when you're guest under my roof, which will be next week. I'm going to barbecue some goats o' Saturday. You and your squaw can come if you like."

Banta chuckled, and for a moment Jim's jaw muscles marbled and he was on the point of stepping into the rancher. But then he said dryly: "Sure, Rube. We'll be there."

Lightfoot signaled that the fun was over by opening the door and herding the others toward it and out into the yard.

You could hear them cackling clean to Sierra County, thought Jim, and he stood there and watched them trudge off to their horses. Back from the darkness came Dave Banta's shout.

"So long, Jim! Hold onto your scalp!"

He went back, ashamed before his wife. He had drunk with these men and fought with one or two, fought beside them during the Texas trail invasion. But by taking a half-breed wife, he had made himself a stranger to them.

Nettie's arms slipped around his neck. She smiled. "It's all right, Jim. They're just testing us."

"It will be all right," said Jim grimly, "if I have to horsewhip every man in Sacaton County."

"What about the women? No, Jim," she said. "If I can't make them respect me for myself, your trouncing them won't help."

That was it, Jim realized. It was something he couldn't fight in the usual way. He snuffed the candle and punched a hole in the bolster for his head. "All right," he said, "I'll keep back. But if the big ox touches you, or his woman says any of the things they're askin' us over to say . . . I'll clean some plows right there."

"It wouldn't help, Jim. We could be proud and lonely, but I don't want to be lonely. I want friends, and friends for our children. I want them coming over to borrow things. I want neighbors, Jim, not next door enemies."

Driving over Saturday morning, Jim kept tucking the blanket about her lap, making sure there wasn't space between them for a thickness of buckskin. It was March, with a few rags of snow under the junipers, brilliant against the red earth. The gray sky was slotted with bars of turquoise. Nettie's coloring was earthy, her lips vivid, her eyes pale blue against dark lashes. Her being so pretty, he thought, would make it no easier for her to get on with the women.

Out under the oaks in Reuben Lightfoot's cañon-bottom home place, the smoke fumed deliciously in barbecue pits. A small army of neighbors had collected—thirty or forty ranchers, their wives, and children. In the rough way of the country, the Lightfoot place was grand. The house was large, a low adobe structure without plaster; the corrals were rambling and tight; there was a barn with a sheet-metal roof.

Rube was the grand and mannerless host, keeping the whiskey flowing while his guests waited for the goats to cook through. Dave Banta lugged a gallon lard can around, smearing tart come-back sauce on the carcasses. Lightfoot roared greetings to the Crofts and a couple of other families just arriving. Mrs. Lightfoot, a small woman with a florid skin and the figure of a sack of potatoes, collected the women.

"Come along and fresh up, ladies," she said. "You might as well come, too, Missus Croft."

Jim stopped dead. He looked at Nettie. It had gone into her like a knife. For an instant he thought she would cry. Then he heard her saying gravely: "I'd like to. Won't you call me Nettie?"

"If you want," said Mrs. Lightfoot coldly.

While she was gone, he toured around among these men he had not seen since his marriage. They all wanted to know where he had captured his squaw, and he told them the same thing: "Off a reservation. Where else?"

"Well, look out for her, ever she goes on the warpath," said tall John Porter.

"Look out for any of them, when that happens," said Jim.

The women came back, and now the barbecue was ready, the savor of it tremendous in the air. Rube stuffed a dish towel under his belt, whipped an edge onto a carving knife, and began to carve. Coffee bubbled endlessly from blackened kettles. Horseshoes *clanged* against a stake somewhere, and men leaned against trees and wagons, with pie tins balanced on their palms. But their eyes were never off Jim and his half-breed wife, and rebellion built steadily in him.

He heard Mrs. Lightfoot say to Nettie: "Tell us about your life at the trading post, girl."

It was suddenly quiet. They waited, like beggars, for the meanest slip they could twist into something laughable or damning.

"Why, it was nice, but lonesome. We'd be snowed in so long, and just the same faces all the time. I was awfully glad when . . . when I came down here. Everyone's been so friendly."

"Did you ever have trouble with . . . with savages?" asked Mrs. Lightfoot.

"Indians, you mean? No, not at our post. They were friendly."

"I expect it's all in knowing how to handle them."

"Yes."

"How do you handle them?" Mrs. Lightfoot asked, and you could hear nothing but a horseshoe *clanging* against an iron stake.

"Just as you'd like to be handled yourself," Nettie said softly.

Mrs. Lightfoot was stopped for a moment. Lucy Banta simpered. "What was your real name, Nettie? Laughing Water, or something?"

One of the younger women tittered. Jim slung his coffee grounds into the pit. The steam flared hotly. He saw Lucy Banta start as he went slowly toward her. "She was born a Christian, Lucy. By the way, I heard they're taking bids for a herd of beef at the territorial prison. You ought to get Dave to bid . . . combine business and pleasure, as you might say."

Mrs. Banta's brother was making hair bridles in Santa Fé, having been caught with a small, select herd of whitefaces two years ago. Nettie arched an alarmed glance at Jim, but he would not back water. He stared Lucy Banta down.

Then he heard Rube Lightfoot's chuckle. "A cow thief," he said, "is just a nester that got caught. That's fine talk from you, squawman."

Jim was seized with a cold and reckless fury. He turned quickly on Lightfoot, gripping the bosom of his buckskin shirt and ramming his back against a tree.

"That's one thing nobody calls me, Rube. Just nobody!"

The rancher grinned, his face larded with a bland satisfaction. "What do we call you . . . gin'ral?"

"Anything except that." Jim was conscious that silence had invaded the yard. Everyone watched. Everyone listened.

Rube gathered his malice in his mouth like spittle. He said softly: "Settin' yourself a big task, Jim, if you aim to whip every man that looks crostwise at you. I figure you don't make a thing something it ain't by telling other folks it's so. If it's there, they'll see it."

"If what's there?"

"What you want them to see."

"I don't want them to see squawman on me, Rube. That's what I'm saying. And you'd better not be talking about anybody else in my family."

The moment was thick; it ended with Mrs. Lightfoot's crying: "Well, land, we ain't touched the pies yet!"

Lightfoot, with a wink at Dave Banta, went to the house. Jim's shoulders made a settling motion, like a dog laying the hairs on his back. He hitched up his belt and looked around. At once he saw that he had blundered. Nettie was biting her lip to keep from crying. He had done what she had begged him not to. He had demanded something that could not be taken by force—respect for his wife. He had, by challenging Rube, merely shamed her. He put aside the rest of his food and went to watch a horseshoe game.

The sun began to drift deeper into the hills. For hours, no one had stopped eating. Most of the men, including Lightfoot, had not stopped drinking. A lot of ranch wives would do the driving on the way home. He had a desperate desire to do something to make amends; he had this desire and at the same time wanted to crush them all with some supreme blow.

As it neared leaving time, Jim became aware that the men were ribbing Lightfoot up to something. When he was drunk, he always did feats of strength. He had already hoisted a calf over his head and wrestled down half the men in sight. Now, with Banta grinning at his side, he swaggered over to Jim.

"Injun rassle you two out of three, gin'ral," he said.

Nettie was shaking her head. Mrs. Lightfoot and the other ladies watched with cockfight eagerness behind their proper faces.

Jim looked Rube over. "Figure you can make it interesting for me?"

"Bet a long yearlin' you won't be bored."

Jim hitched up his pants and lay on the ground. Loaded with food and liquor, Lightfoot arranged his arms and legs for the best purchase. The men swarmed around them as they raised their legs on signal and began sparring. Rattlesnake quick, Jim's foot caught Lightfoot's ankle. A single heave threw the rancher out of position.

Jim laughed, while Rube swore and began claiming he had not been ready. Dave Banta laughed. "Ready as you'd ever be, Rube. Tally one for Jim."

Lightfoot's face was swollen with fury. He lay back. Banta called time and their legs went up. Cagey this time, Lightfoot feinted. Abruptly locking his knee about Jim's leg, he gave a sideward yank. Jim turned his leg and let the man's weight slough aside. With a surprised gasp, Rube rocked onto his side. He grunted—"Anybody can run!"—and began to spar again.

Immediately Jim caught the fat leg with his heel and threw Lightfoot onto his face.

He sprang up. Banta and the others hooted at the rancher's protests. Lightfoot came up, looking sick and ugly.

"I hope all your kids are born with feathers in their hair, Croft," he said.

For a moment, Jim could almost feel his pulpy mouth on his knuckles. But after a moment his rage drained out of him. He was tired and defeated. He turned away, hating them all. He hated each one and he hated them as a clan. He despised them for the lonely years ahead of Nettie. Remembering about the Tres Piedras pasture, he knew what he was going to say. He would tell Rube to keep the hell out, or there would be shooting trouble.

He was glad when the day finally ended. Darkness stifled the big ranch yard. Children began to fuss and livestock bawled in the pasture. Jim went to collect the pans in which Nettie had brought gooseberry pies. He found them in the kitchen, returning then to look for Nettie. But she had gone to the wagon in the trees.

As he entered the dark grove, Jim heard scuffling. He halted, listening. Nettie's voice came, low and taut. "Mister Lightfoot! You aren't yourself."

The rancher's voice was choked with heat. "Don't be coy with old Rube, gal. I know Injun gals. Come on, now. . . ."

Jim was striding through the dark. He heard Nettie sobbing with hurt and shame: "Mister Lightfoot!"

Lightfoot was a hunched, bearish back. All Jim could see of Nettie was her face over his shoulder. Rube's mouth was pressed against the hollow of her throat. At the last instant he heard Jim. He swerved away and came slowly about. Jim's fist collided with his cheek bone. It made a sharp, meaty *slap.*

Rube reeled back against a wagon shaft. Nettie cried out and came between them. The horse reared. Thrusting her aside, Jim met the rancher. Lightfoot's fist boomed against his chest. Jim hit him a savage chop on the ear. Lightfoot was driven to the ground, but he seized Jim's legs and pulled himself up.

A lantern was swinging in quick arcs through the trees. "What's all the rannikaboo, there, Rube?" someone shouted. Mrs. Lightfoot's cry came with a lacing of fear: "Reuben!"

Jim squared off, his fist cocked. Rube's face was a blank, bruised target. He looked scared. Jim savored the moment. Lightfoot had had his day of shaming others, and now he was about to be shamed before his wife and guests. He would never again ride into town without seeing hands raised to whispering mouths.

But it was suddenly Nettie's face before Jim, and her hands were against his chest. "No, Jim!" she said urgently. Jim thrust her away. "Jim, please! For me! You promised. . . ."

When Dave Banta arrived to hold his lantern above the men and the girl and the rearing horse, Jim stood with his long arms hanging. Rube looked drunk and foolish. The tableau lingered until Mrs. Lightfoot and the rest crowded in. Jim saw the shame and terror in her face. He was oddly touched—troubled that she must suffer, too.

Abruptly Nettie turned toward Rube. She touched his bruised cheek bone, exclaiming in sympathy,

"Oh, it's going to blacken, Rube! We're so sorry. Jim," she cried, "I asked you not to use that horse! Why, he's just a half-trained bronc'!"

Jim was stopped. Nettie pulled Rube away from the shafts. Dave Banta seized the cheek strap to drag the horse down.

"Look out for him," Nettie cautioned. "He's a terror to club you with his head. Why, Rube was just harnessing him for me and he hit him without blinking an eye. He hit Jim only last week. On . . . on the right ear, wasn't it, Jim?"

Nettie's eyes were begging him. "The left," said Jim. "I wouldn't've taken him, only he was handy. Rube, I reckon I owe you an apology." His mouth barely smiled.

Rube stirred out of his paralysis. "Sho', I ought to know a skittish horse when I see one. My fault, Jim."

His wife, thought Jim, had the eyes of a grateful dog. She was looking gently at Nettie. "Don't feel sorry for the man," she said. "Maybe the horse just knows a drunken old fool when it sees one."

Jim shouted his laughter, and that was the end of it. Rube took their banter, fussed with the harness, and finally the four of them were alone. Jim tucked the robe about Nettie, straight and dark-haired on the seat. As he put his foot up to mount, Mrs. Lightfoot spoke hesitantly. "He . . . he does the most outlandish things when he's drinking, Nettie."

"Your husband's a great one to chivaree, that's all. He might have fooled me, only Jim told me beforehand . . . 'Rube's a great josher. But he's got a heart as good as gold.' "

"Did Jim say that? Well, Rube's a diamond in the rough, only sometimes. . . ."

Just as the wagon ground away, Rube called: "You go ahead and use that pasture, Jim! What's the use of good neighbors argifying over a little old buck pasture like that 'un?"

In the darkness, Nettie's eyes met Jim's, moist and laughing, and Jim knew it was over. They would come no more in the night, insinuating and trying them. When they came, it would be as friends.

★ ★ ★ ★ ★

Blood on the Bozeman Trail

★ ★ ★ ★ ★

I

Sam Cary left the interior of the yellow railroad station and paused a moment in the doorway before stepping into the sunlight. He was tall and limber-muscled, wearing a softly tanned leather shirt and old cavalry breeches with stripes of darker blue where the yellow slashes had been removed. His flat Stetson was worn forward and to one side, a hat with its own casualness, the color of the deserts.

Glancing about him, he breathed the hot smell of the prairie town. Before him, the steel tracks glistened under the sun. A handcar was drawn up beside the ties and at the corner of the station an Indian pony scratched luxuriously against a wooden sign nailed to the building. Cary's glance went briefly beyond it, to his own wagon camp a short distance away. A man on horseback rode into the sprawling square of wagons, dragging a load of mesquite roots by a rope. Bullwhackers worked stolidly in the morning heat, putting down the last of the freight for the haul from this railroad town of Cheyenne to Cary's trading post on the Montana border.

Cary turned to watch two of his teamsters back-and-bellying a crate from the loading dock, noting that four barrels still remained. Again he glanced at the camp, saw no one coming for the barrels, and stepped into the sunlight and crossed the tracks. Vaulting up on the high dock, he frowned at the words he had chalked on the tops of the barrels: *Donovan Repack*. Looking up, he saw his wagon master, John Silvertooth, coming from the

115

camp. Cary dropped to the ground and walked to meet him. The scorch of heated earth went through his boot soles. The sun was like yellow glass melting in the sky. The thick, blackstrap odor of sage was in the air. Reaching Silvertooth, Cary asked offhandedly: "Where's Donovan?"

Silvertooth took time to fill his pipe. He was a big man in a red miner's shirt and smoke-tanned buckskin trousers. Deep grooves of displeasure pinched the skin between his eyes. "Ain't seen him since breakfast," he said. "I hear it took six men to put him out of The Nations last night. If he's got a hangover the size of his drunk, he'll sweat boilermakers for a week."

They walked toward camp. At the forge wagon, a shirtless workman struck a rosy ox shoe with ringing echoes.

Sam Cary stopped in the shade of a tall freight wagon. There was no sign of activity at Donovan's faded blue Murphy wagon. Crates and barrels stood about and the tailgate was down. Cary took a long breath of dissatisfaction.

Silvertooth heard it and spat a mouthful of smoke. "I say he's a troublemaker by trade. I could find a dozen better than him in any saloon."

"Soberer, maybe," Cary agreed. "But oxen and Ogallalas don't set much store by whether or not a man's taken the pledge. Once we leave town, he won't be finding a saloon at every corner."

"If we leave town," said the wagon master.

"We always have, haven't we?"

"Up to now. But these bullwhackers are spoiling faster than pork, and the pork smells to high heaven. They had an edge like a Green River knife a week ago. They'd had their fun and were set to go. Now they've lost it."

Cary leaned by one elbow against a wheel a foot taller than he was. "They'll get it back fast enough, once they're standing night guard in Sioux country."

Disgruntlement did not leave Silvertooth's eyes. "Not with an Irishman like Donovan bragging of what he's getting away with. Castro came to me this morning and asked could he pay back his advance and go out with Mark Stockwell's outfit. Stockwell got here three days after us, and he's going out before."

"What did you tell him?"

Silvertooth glanced at a cut knuckle. "I told him, no. There won't any more of them ask it, but I don't like the look of it. That mick put him up to it. The same as he came to you and offered to sign on if you'd loan him the money to buy out of the Army."

"Still a bargain," Cary stated. "He can't stand freedom. That's all that ails Donovan. Once we stretch out, he'll pay his way."

"I don't like gambling on 'whackers. Not this year. This is the Sioux' year. The year of the big hunt. We should have gone out a week ago, when the men were standing on their hind legs clawing at the sky."

Cary smiled. "Don't blame me. I only own half this outfit. The other half will be here tomorrow sure . . . if the train doesn't get stamped by a herd of buffalo."

He found a dipper on a nail and raised the lid of a barrel lashed to the side of the wagon. Pouring a dipperful in his hat, he set it on the ground to soak. He drank a dipperful, letting it slide tepidly over his chest and puddle above his belt. Then he poured the water out of his hat and glanced up to see Silvertooth frowning at him.

"Are you going to let Gaybird go with us?"

For a moment Cary's mouth got tight. He regarded the other man flatly. "What have I got to say about it? She's of age."

"She's your ward, ain't she?"

"At eighteen? She can sign checks now, and pick a husband. She'll be making her own decisions." He frowned. "Though, of course, I mean to throw the fear into her about the trail."

"I'd think so," said Silvertooth pompously. "If I was you, I'd say to her . . . 'Look here! That Bozeman road ain't no doings for a white man any more, let alone a woman. You get on that train tomorrow and go back to Cincinnati!' Though I don't expect she'll be fighting to live in a wagon anyhow, after the seminary."

Cary smiled. "You're talking about handling squaws and horses, John. Gaybird isn't quite either. She's cold-jawed as a bronc' and smart as a young squaw. She'll want to be handled cleverly." Carefully he set his hat over his eye. They left the shade of the wagon. "I thought of buying her out," he explained. "Her dad's half interest ought to be worth fifteen thousand by now. I could give notes."

"She couldn't live on notes."

"I've got some cash."

"None you don't need. You owe Bill Orrum two thousand on those rifles." Then Silvertooth looked startled and glanced about to be sure no one had followed, trade arms being banned on the Bozeman road this year. He referred to the code word, more loudly than was necessary. "I say, you need two thousand to pay for that hardware."

"God forbid I should ever need you for a spy." Cary chuckled. "I could give her some cash now and a thousand or so at the end of the summer. It's not right she should go into that Indian warren again. That was all right for her dad, and for a girl of thirteen. It was peaceful, then, part of the time, anyway. But she's no child, now. She'd find it rough."

Silvertooth tamped the hot, gray tobacco with his thumb. "She didn't find it rough last time she was out. She was riding everything in the corral. She learned to talk Ogallala with the wash women."

"That," Cary pointed out, "was summer before last. She was

sixteen. There's a difference between a girl of sixteen and one of eighteen."

Silvertooth thought, and nodded, and said: "Yes, I reckon there is."

Cary had the nostalgic feeling that he would never see her again, the curious, laughing little girl animal with black pigtails who Old Bob Phillips had left him to raise five years ago. A freighting accident had ended Cary and Phillips's partnership in Fort Graybull a year after they built it. Cary had installed the girl in a seminary in Cincinnati; summers, she visited the post.

On her last visit, two years ago, she had been a fascinating half-civilized creature of sixteen. But Indian smokes had fumed too steadily last summer, and he had instructed her not to come out. He had again advised it this spring, but now it was June and he had her letter saying she would be out, and please wait for her in Cheyenne when he made up his annual freight train. He would wait, of course, but she could not make him take her. A man must go by his judgment, and Sam Cary himself was returning to the Bighorn country only because his trade forced him to.

They crossed the camp through the jungle of trash, tarpaulins, and tar buckets to Donovan's wagon and trailer outfit. Silvertooth looked about. He said bitterly: "Look at that!"

In the slovenliness of the wagon there was offense to a wagon master. The tailgate slouched against a wheel and crates sat about in total lack of order. A rack of lead-lined yokes was overturned by the wagon. Silvertooth's hand angrily swept a heap of pipe dottle from the wagon bed. "Damned if he ain't trying to burn the outfit up now!"

Cary recalled a conversation with Tom Braga, who ran The Nations saloon. He said thoughtfully: "Braga was talking about a shotgun the other day. Donovan had been raising a little hell the night before. Pig knuckles brine all over the nude behind the bar. A shame, at that. Braga was fond of that picture, and now the lady's left breast has run."

Silvertooth squinted with a tart blue eye. "A shotgun, eh? On one of our boys?"

Cary shrugged. "Talk. Donovan didn't have any money, did he?" His glance went curiously to Silvertooth.

Color invaded Silvertooth's face. "Not honest to God money, I reckon. I gave him four-bits for a pick-me-up after breakfast. He was shaking like a Cheyenne pup in February. But on four-bits he couldn't raise a smile."

Cary regarded him frowningly and began to walk back toward the tracks. After a moment Silvertooth followed. "Listen," he said, "he couldn't get in trouble on four-bits."

"After last night he could get in trouble by just showing his Irish face in The Nations."

"He knows better than that . . . don't he?" Silvertooth demanded.

"Maybeso. I keep thinking about that nude."

They reached the tracks and gazed up the dusty main street. Horses, turnouts, and pedestrians briskly came and went through the rutted avenue cutting across the casual sprawl of tents, frame buildings, and brick structures. "Well, we'll take a look," Cary said.

They crossed the tracks and passed the big trail outfit from Fort Stockwell, Montana Territory—Mark Stockwell's trading post in the Gallatin Valley. With dissatisfaction, Cary noted that a number of Stockwell's wagons were sheeted and ready to move. And they'd arrived after Cary.

Silvertooth observed this, also, and commented sourly: "He's worked the tallow out of his boys to hit the road ahead of us. If he takes out first, we'll live in his dust and camp trash and drink the brine he leaves in the water holes all the way back to the border."

"Maybe his mules will all come down with the swinney," Cary said. "Not that I wish him bad luck."

They moved into town. Cary kept to the thin slice of shade against the buildings. The sun, reflecting from the bleached ground, pinched his eyes. Freight outfits whooped and lurched along the shallow cañon of the street. Railroad workers were everywhere, hard-bitten Irishmen on their way to end of track or heading back from it. Soldiers from Fort Russell sauntered about. Distantly a smith's sledge shaped a tire to a wheel bound for the wilderness.

This was still a town of primary colors and emotions, running more to tent and frame than to brick, more to fights than discussions. In this vigorous emotional climate, gunsmiths outthrove haberdashers, and saloonkeepers prospered above all others. Donovan might be in any of twenty saloons, spending his fifty cents on beer or hunting whiskey credit. They glanced into the Shamrock, but the bullwhacker's bearish shoulders were not at the bar. They tried the Copperopolis. Donovan had not been seen.

Moving on, they investigated the Pawnee Bar. The Irishman was not at the bar, but as they went out the door, a lean, dark-skinned man in stained buckskins collided with them. He wore a round-crowned Stetson, from which pigtails descended, tied with greasy rawhide bows. Cary stared past him but the newcomer said with a grin: "Howdy, Cary! Are you early or am I late?"

Cary said: "We're both early. I'll see you later, Orrum. In front of Bailey's."

Bill Orrum saluted and stood aside, a tall and indolent man with a fondness for rings and Indian tobacco. Silvertooth did not hide his dislike for the man as they passed; he failed to speak, and, after they were on the walk, he growled at Cary: "You're not parading around with that offscraping right in the open, are you?"

"He's got guns," Cary said shortly. "If the Army won't let us buy them openly, we'll buy them in back lots and carry them under bolts of cloth. I don't know whether they're more afraid of the guns falling into the hands of Indians, or of honest traders making a dollar. We aren't going back into the Sioux country with the kind of blunderbusses the 'whackers are carrying."

Silvertooth grunted. "The smell of him will rub off onto you if anybody sees you talking to him. He ain't going up the Bozeman with us, is he?"

"No. I take delivery of the guns in the brush."

They had drinks at the Shamrock, after failing to locate Donovan in any of the larger bars. He had not been at The Nations, and Cary found the edge of his concern dulling. Afterward, Silvertooth went up the street on business of his own. Cary consulted his watch. It was time now for his meeting with Bill Orrum. Yet he did not hurry. He had another drink, wanting savagely to persuade Orrum that they had nothing in common beyond a mutual interest in contraband weapons. Orrum was a shotgun trader, a smuggler of whiskey into Indian Territory, and the operator of a sporting house in Bannock. It was a demeaning thing to trade with him, but necessity had shaped many a man's ethics before Cary's.

In front of Bailey's Hardware, a collection of crates partially blocked the board sidewalk. Bill Orrum's crow-like shape was balanced on a crate as Cary approached. He was in conversation with another man. Cary hesitated. It would not do to seem to have an appointment with him. Orrum's trade was too well known. The Army was lackadaisically inspecting all wagons going north on the Bozeman, but friends of Orrum's ran the risk of a more careful inspection.

Orrum's round-crowned Stetson hung between his shoulder blades by the rawhide lanyard. His black braids glistened with grease. His head obscured the face of the other man, so that Cary had approached to within twenty feet when the trader leaned back, exposing the face of Mark Stockwell.

Cary's inclination was to pass them up. But Orrum glanced around at a word from Stockwell, and his deep, slow voice said: "You've kept me waiting."

Cary put a boot sole against a crate, a dry disgust in his eyes. "Well, you see, I was up with a sick teamster," he said. "You seem to be in good company, anyhow."

Orrum smoked a red Indian pipe and regarded Cary lazily. Smoking enough *shongsasha* in time wrapped a man in an aura of wildness, as his buckskins took on the wilderness stain of buffalo grease and wood smoke. Orrum had acquired this fragrance. He wore Blackfoot moccasins and was somber and sparing of humor.

"I could teach you things about freighting," he remarked. "One of them is not to hire a crew till you're ready to stretch. 'Whackers spoil faster than venison once they've taken the notion to travel. I hear your outfit's falling apart."

Mark Stockwell's pottery-brown eyes smiled. "Sam's in no condition to travel anyway, Bill. He's expecting. Every year about this time he becomes a father for the summer. He's got a black-haired ward with a waist you could span with your two hands." He laughed and punched Cary. Big and heavy-boned, durable as a Murphy wagon, Stockwell had a rugged countenance with a strong ledge of bone over the eyes. His shoulders filled his brown blanket coat and his neck was short and strong.

"When's she coming in?" Orrum asked carelessly.

"Tomorrow."

"Is she going up to the fort with you?" Stockwell demanded.

"Hard to say."

"If she were my ward, it wouldn't be hard. The Sioux are hunting early, like they had a big show planned for fall. We didn't lose sight of their smoke till we left the Bighorns."

Orrum sipped smoke from the pipe. "I reckon you boys could cut some throats in Washington for abandoning the Bozeman posts, eh?"

Stockwell shrugged. "They were blunderers, but they might have blundered in sometime when we wanted them. Still . . . I keep the Injuns buttered up."

Cary regarded him quietly. "With ninety-proof butter? You're new to The Nations, Mark. I don't know how it was with you in New Mexico, but up here a man who buys the Indians' friendship with whiskey is chiseling his own headstone. When you take it away from them, you'll have a chivaree on your hands."

Stockwell smiled. "Maybe I won't take it away from them. I tease them. A bottle now, a bottle then. It gets me bargains when they come to trade. And I see to it that they do their drinking away from the post."

Orrum exhaled a grayness of bitter smoke. "I wonder how come the Army to pull out? They lost a hundred and fifty men holding the posts last summer. Then they pulled out. Does that make sense?"

"Why do they wear winter uniforms until the men drop from the heat?" Cary said. "Because the head of the brute is in Washington, and the tail's in Wyoming. They'll let a trader build his post in the Sioux country on the proposition that he'll have protection. Then they walk out on him, and the trade dries up. Mark and I are the army, this season."

Black as currants, Orrum's eyes crinkled. "Or you might say you are, Sam. Mark had the good sense to build in Montana."

Stockwell's good humor thinned to a pinch at the corners of his mouth. "Don't hold it against me that the Army pulled out on you," he said. "You talked it around that I was a fool to build my post where I did. You thought you'd grab off all the trade bound for the Montana mines before it ever reached me.

For a while, you nearly did. The point is, I saw the time coming when the Army would pull out and the travel would steer away from the Bozeman. The Bighorns have been Sioux country for centuries. It's the last big hunting ground, and you know and I know and the Army knows that they won't give it up without a scrap. So the Army gave up." With a gold cigar cutter, he trimmed a cigar. He roasted it in a match flame, and, when Cary said nothing, merely watching him with a curious, half-amused light in his eyes, he said: "So now the traffic goes north and east of us, by Missouri River packet. But they still come down from the mines to trade with Mark Stockwell. The lesson in it is . . . never trust the Army."

"Isn't that the lesson for both of us?" Cary pointed out. "When they man the forts again, you'll be swapping trade beads to squaws for coyote pelts. Just when you expect the Army least, they'll come back."

Stockwell said dryly: "Let's all hope they come back. There's room for both of us. We can be rivals, can't we, without being enemies?"

"I've always thought so." Cary smiled.

The trader made a place for himself on the walk, moving unhurriedly toward the foot of town.

Cary then stared quickly and without rancor at Bill Orrum.

"We'll come to that," Orrum said. "Walk up to my camp with me." Sam watched him strike his pipe against a crate. *He's more like an Indian than Crazy Dog himself,* Sam thought. *He's got the wild smell, the pigtails, the dark and greasy look.*

Orrum's way was to bring in ten or fifteen wagons loaded with what he could sell quickly, dispose of it along with the wagons, and leave himself encumbered only with gold. His camp was in a coulée west of town, and consisted of a bedroll, a deer-hide tent, one wagon, three span of oxen, and a riding mule. He had jerked venison drying on a line, and yanked off a strip and tossed it to Cary. Cary held it but did not eat; it was easier to tell a man he was a liar and a thief than to say his food was filthy.

From the tent, Orrum procured a rifle. He drew it and laid his cheek against the stock, sighting briefly and letting the hammer *snick*. "Springfield-Allin," he said. "Trapdoor Springfield."

It had a grand balance in Cary's hands. It was snug and compact, and so new the grease had not all been rubbed off. He sighted and let the hammer drop. Quickly he re-cocked and threw open the trap-door breech. The gun was at his cheek again in three seconds.

"This is the one," he breathed. His hand rubbed the brass lock plate.

"One hundred Springfield-Allins," said Orrum, chewing the jerky. "Same price, forty dollars apiece, cash. Four thousand. . . ."

Cary's eyes snapped. "*Half* cash! The rest at the end of the season. That was the bargain."

Orrum shrugged. "That was before we knew how bad things was. When they massacred them miners last month, I got to thinking all cash might be a better idea. I hear, too, they put an arrow in John Silvertooth's rump at Old Woman Creek on your way down."

"Did you, now?" Cary said.

Orrum recovered the gun. Putting it back in the tent, he said: "No matter, Sam. I can sell 'em."

Cary's hand pulled him around and there was a meaty slap as his palm wiped across the gunrunner's cheek. "You're not going to hedge on me! I had the money brought up from Denver, but half of it goes into supplies."

Orrum's eyes snapped blackly as he stood under the pressure of Cary's hand. "I owe every dollar I'll get out of this to the bank. I can get the cash from somebody else if I can't from you.

I'm traveling north with Stockwell. I reckon he'd buy them in a minute."

"How much," Cary asked, "is he paying you to hold me up?"

"You wouldn't think much of me if I told my customers' names, would you, Sam?" Orrum smiled.

"I don't think much of you . . . put it that way. Where are the guns?"

Orrum grinned. "Where's the four thousand?" He turned away to build a fire under a kettle. "I'll be around The Nations till ten o'clock. After that, I don't know where I'll be. But somebody else will have the map of where I left the guns."

Cary pulled a buckskin whang from the yoke of his shirt. His hands tugged on it a moment before it snapped. He threw the pieces in the fire. He said: "I'll draw the money out of the bank today and leave it at The Nations. Where's the map of your cache?"

Orrum grinned, and from his shirt he pulled a small patch of rawhide. On it he had drawn a map of where the guns were hidden. "They're in Sweetwater Coulée," he said. "Oxen chained to the wheels. A night's drive in, but start early if you want to beat the sun."

Cary put the rawhide inside his own shirt. "Thanks," he said, and his shoulder moved and Orrum ducked too late. The fist cracked against his cheek bone. He stumbled against his tent and fell. He lay there with his black eyes dull and evil as those of a sand rattler. He said: "I'll remember that."

Cary's shoulders moved. "Fine. Now we've both got something to remember."

It was mid-afternoon when he sauntered down the street, but it had not cooled. The heat made a man think of liquids; Cary let his glance travel downstreet. A burly figure in a red shirt approached through the turmoil of boardwalk traffic, moving quickly, and Cary suddenly saw that it was his wagon master.

"One of the 'whackers just came in," Silvertooth said. "He says Donovan tried to borrow money from him."

"Did he let him have it?"

"No. But Donovan said he was going to have his liquor at The Nations or wreck the place. He's down the street."

Cary frowningly hitched up his belt. Both men stopped across the street from the big false-fronted saloon. In the stifling afternoon, horses crowded the unbarked hitch racks. Now a great-shouldered shape of a man lounged from the foot of town and stopped before the slotted doors of the saloon. The sun burned in Donovan's crisp red hair. Cary saw him glance down at his palm, toss a coin on it, and with resolution move into the saloon.

"The crazy mick," Silvertooth breathed.

Cary called out, but the doors had closed behind the freighter. They crossed the street. Cary stroked the slotted doors aside and glanced into the saloon. There was a feeling of lassitude in the huge, rough room with its mud walls and black-iron chandeliers. Customers were plentiful, but it was early for celebrating. Dice bounced, cards flashed, a soprano voice shrill with whiskey was singing "Oh, Willie, We Have Missed You". Behind the bar was Braga's notorious nude, an opulent lithograph of a naked woman recumbent on a field of leopard skin. Brine of pig's knuckles had smeared her bosom.

Donovan was moving along the bar, his figure wreathed in tobacco fumes. He was a black Irishman of rough make and blunt terra-cotta features. He shouldered into an opening and struck his coin against the varnished pine. A barkeeper stopped and placed both hands on the bar.

"I'm hot, thirsty, and broke," Donovan said with desperate cheerfulness. "Give me a shot of the worst whiskey in the place, and faith knows the best is bad enough."

The barman was glancing about for Tom Braga. Cary moved inside, seeing Braga come from the rear. When he swung past a table, Cary saw the bung-starter in his hip pocket. He was a grossly fat man with a body shaped like a sack of potatoes. Cary had no use for him. His anxiety to be catering to other men's appetites glistened on him like sweat.

Donovan heard Braga approaching and turned to meet him. He did something that showed Sam Cary how desperate he was. He offered his hand to Braga. He said: "No hard feelings?"

Braga's hands rested on his hips. "No," he said. "But no whiskey, either." He smiled.

Donovan turned resignedly to the barkeeper. "A beer, then."

He slowly turned back as Braga said levelly: "And no beer."

Cary said from the door: "Is this any way to treat an old customer, Braga? Who's drunk more of your rotgut than Donovan? And it's pretty bum rotgut."

Braga's head turned. "Rotgut! My whiskey is bonded. . . ." He observed Cary's smile and amended: "Anyway, it is good, for Cheyenne. Good enough for swilling."

"Then you can handle the by-products of swilling, such as ruined dispositions."

Donovan's voice was a growl. "Will you let me handle my own affairs, Cary? I'm buying for myself, right?"

"Wrong," Braga said.

Donovan's hand massaged the half dollar. "I'm not a regular drunkard, man! I thought I was going out today and it would be my last drunk. But Mister Cary has decided to let us rot in Cheyenne a while longer. And the gods know I'm wanting a drink!"

Braga's glistening eyes savored the situation. "That's fine. Do your drinking at the Copperopolis, then. Or have they had enough of you, too?"

Donovan made a gesture of wiping his jaws with his palm.

"No liquor, hey?"

"Not a drop. Get out."

"Damn you!" Donovan roared it. "You'd let a man shake the hand of pig like you and then deny him a drink!" The back of his hand smashed across Braga's mouth, rocking his head. He turned, took hold of a beer cask in its cradle on the bar, and swung it about. Cutting the spigot open, he sank to his knees and let the foaming column spill into his mouth. Braga lunged back, the bung-starter in his hand. He swung at Donovan's head, and Donovan raised an arm and half warded the blow. It landed with force enough to drop him to the floor.

Cary moved in quickly. They came from four points, the dish-toweled barmen armed with lengths of pool cue. It was neatly planned, smoothly executed, and the only unplanned factors appeared to be Cary and John Silvertooth.

"Braga!" Cary shouted.

Leaning over the bullwhacker with the mallet raised, Braga halted. He discovered the stein Cary had thrown at him. He ducked. It smashed into his shoulder, drenching him with beer.

Cary lunged into him, his eyes on Braga's pulpy mouth. His fist collided with it with the good smack of a hand laid on a quarter of beef. Braga reeled into a table.

Cary heard a saloon man slide in behind him. A lamp cast the shadow of an arm. A houseman, short and deep-chested and with a red, congested face, chopped savagely at Cary's head with a truncated pool cue. Cary fell away, raising his shoulder defensively. The club struck painfully against the bunched muscle. Cary set his teeth and lunged into the man. He caught the thick, corded throat with his hands, jammed him against the tall bar, and hacked at the turgid face with the edge of his knuckles. The saloon man shouted and tried to writhe away. Cary gathered the power of his back and shoulder muscles in an overhand blow that smashed into the side of the man's jaw and turned it. He let the white face slide away.

The saloon crowd had shaped into a random crescent with Donovan, Cary, and Silvertooth in the center and three of Braga's men carefully working in with pool cue clubs at the ready. Cary looked at the ring of faces behind this shock troop, thinking of loafer wolves. A tall man with a sallow, hairless face slanted in to chop at Donovan's head. Donovan caught the club in his hand, ripped it away, and smashed the man across the nose. The houseman went to his knees, covering his face with his hands. Donovan bent, seized him by an arm and a leg, and lifted him over his head. He crouched and straightened, hurling the man across the counter and into the stacked bottles of the backbar. He took time to seize Cary by the arm, then, his face dark with anger he said: "Get out of it! I can handle six of their likes alone!"

"Can you handle one with a scatter-gun?" Silvertooth panted.

Donovan's bloodshot eyes comprehended slowly. He looked around for Tom Braga, but the saloonkeeper had disappeared. Donovan stood slope-shouldered and puzzled.

Now Cary heard a man and saw him fall back in the crowd and turn to thrust to the rear. It was like a signal, splitting the crowd and folding it back to front and rear; men were shouting their terror, and one raised an arm toward Cary as if to ward off a blow. Cary suddenly brought his fist down at the root of Donovan's neck, carrying him to the floor with him. He saw Braga's men fall back, getting out of line. It placed Tom Braga directly behind him, behind the bar, moving in with his double-barreled shotgun.

Cary crouched there, his hand grasping at the sawdust. Donovan was shouting curses and reaching for the edge of the bar. Cary rose suddenly and Braga was before him; a squat and greasy-faced man with a side-hammer shotgun prodding forward. Cary slapped his left hand down on the gun barrel.

His right hand flung sawdust into the saloon man's face. He felt the shattering roar of the gun through his hand and arm. The charge flashed between him and Donovan. Overhead, the candles puffed out. Lamps burned at front and rear, and in the gloom men were lying on their bellies and clutching at the floor.

Braga wrenched at the gun, his face distorted. Cary's hand slapped down on the hammers. He brought the gun barrel up and around and Braga's grip was broken. Cary emptied the other charge into the ceiling. As he threw the gun aside, he saw Donovan vault the bar and trap Tom Braga against the backbar. He saw his fist come back and drive in, cock and drive again, his head held slightly on the side. He watched Donovan release him. Braga turned and took one blind step toward the end of the bar, and collapsed.

Donovan turned back. The saloon was quiet. Donovan moved along the bar to the front, took a final look at the saloon, and moved into the street. Cary and his wagon master lingered a moment and followed him.

Donovan was waiting on the walk. He said: "I suppose I should thank you, Mister Cary?"

"I'd thank God, if I were you," Cary said. "Did you get your fill of beer?"

"I got more than that. I got a fist into the middle of a face I've been aching to spoil. But it's too bad it had to end the way it did."

"How's that?"

"With me beholden to you."

Smiling, Cary watched Donovan shoulder into the crowd gathering before the saloon.

Silvertooth had a puffiness under his eye and his calico shirt was ripped. Sourly he observed Donovan's departure. "I could do with a whiskey, unless you're afraid I'd be throwing pig's knuckles at somebody's nude."

"You'd be more likely," Cary said, "to be throwing looks at her."

II

The day finished out in a red and gritty dusk. Cary intended waiting for dark before leaving for the rifle cache. Supper fires puddled the dusk of the corral. A teamster was frying venison in a long-handled iron skillet. From south of town, the day guard rode in from herding stock.

It was all rough and casual, all utterly masculine. Cary remembered how Gaybird Phillips used to drink the strong liquor of bullwhackers' yarns. How would it all seem to her now, a grown woman, after two years away from unshaven jowls, lumbering wagons, and dust—fine dust, coarse dust, red dust, and black dust?

He regarded her Dearborn wagon, standing spruce-topped among the burly freight wagons on the south line. A thought came to him. Presently he walked to his own wagon and struck a match. He grubbed in the catch-all box at the rear of it. He found something, and slipped it into his pocket with the map. Moving silently, he mounted the ladder at the back of the Dearborn.

As he stepped through the flap, he heard a quick intake of breath. Cary's hand dropped to the warm smoothness of brass and walnut at his thigh. In the gloom, John Silvertooth spoke quickly: "Now behave! I was just checking around."

Cary lit the lamp. The light sparkled on a pair of beaded gauntlets in the wagon master's hand. "I see."

In an excess of casualness, Silvertooth tossed them on the cot. "First of these I ever seen that anybody but a muleskinner could wear. Thought she'd like them."

Cary took a pair of moccasins from his pocket and laid them on the bed. "I thought the same when I saw these Blackfoot moccasins. She always did favor them. I was wondering if that squaw got her sheets clean."

He pulled back the red-and-gray Indian blanket and inspected the stiff cotton sheets.

"What's the difference?" Silvertooth grunted. "She ain't going up with us."

"But she'll have a day or two in town."

They moved about, hunting dust and insects. The wagon contained a small chest, a commode, a goose-feather cot, a chair, and a mirror. Cary moved to the flap, and the wagon master said quickly: "She comes tomorrow, eh?"

"You know that."

"I thought you maybe had something to tell me."

"Why should I have?"

Silvertooth said: "All right, I'll tell you something. The first summer she came out after you put her in the seminary, she told my missus something. She was fifteen, warn't she? She said you and her was married. She said to keep it secret."

Cary's lips parted. He set them firmly together and his hand rubbed his thigh. "She did, eh?"

"She did."

"How many washwomen has your wife told that to?"

"You know the answer to that. What I want to know is, what are you going to do about her?"

Cary found his pipe and packed it; he put it unlighted into his mouth. "Well, just so you won't think it's worse than it is . . . you see, I never figured we were married. Old Bob Phillips made me promise to adopt her if anything happened to him. After that freighting accident did for him, I took her to Cincinnati. But it seems bachelors weren't adopting fourteen-year-old girls that year. I tried to set her in the seminary, but they reckoned that would make a kept woman out of her. So all I could do was marry her. Then I enrolled her in the school as

Missus Samuel Cary."

"That's about how I laid it out," the wagon master said. "Still, that was then. What about now?"

Cary lighted the pipe. "I've heard Eastern women wear bleaching towels over their faces to keep their skin white. Gaybird will be a real Eastern lady. She'll take one look at the grease stains on my shirt and lose color. It will be an annulment or a divorce."

From the distant Laramie Hills, night sprawled across the prairie. They rode into the stiff rabbitbrush, walking their mounts until they were clear of Stockwell's camp, a hundred yards west, and then letting them reach.

They put ten miles behind them, miles as devoid of individuality as the ties of the tracks they followed. But as they rode, they looked about often, holding their ponies in to listen. Farther north, anywhere beyond the Platte, a night ride would be suicide. Down here there was chiefly the possibility of encountering a band of Ogallala Sioux out cutting telegraph wires.

A kangaroo rat bounded from the path of Cary's pony with a frightened chirp. The horse swerved; Cary hauled it around with an oath. He found he had flung his carbine up automatically.

Northwest he made out the flat bulk of a range of hills. The landmark placed them a mile or so east of Sweetwater Coulée. According to Orrum's map, the wagon ought to be about two miles south of the tracks, hidden in the coulée.

Silvertooth glanced at him. "Am I gettin' womanly," he asked, "or do I smell Sioux?"

"You're gettin' womanly." Cary's horse shook bridle with a *jingle* of coin silver. The wind was redolent of sage. They dipped into a wallow and mounted again the dead level of the plain.

Cary grunted. "Hope the fool left the oxen on a stout picket."
Silvertooth's arm went up. "Yonder they are."

"Crafty like a fool quail." Sam snorted. "Hide the wagons
and leave the oxen in sight! Hell, there's three span of them."

They made it to be about two hundred feet to the gully on
the bank of which stood the animals. Cary was on the point of
touching his horse with his heels when suddenly his right arm
extended to touch Silvertooth.

Silvertooth sat steadily in the saddle, staring. They saw one of
the animals on the coulée's edge raise its head for an instant,
scent, and quietly go back to pulling tufts of grass. It was light
enough to determine that they were not oxen. Nor did they
carry saddles. They were Indian ponies.

The two men turned silently and retreated. Dismounting,
Cary thumbed back the heavy spur of the bronze-framed Henry.
Big John Silvertooth moored his calico mule to a clump of
black sage. He removed his hat and dropped it on the ground.
A bare head was his fighting trim.

Cary stared at the Indian ponies in the far darkness. The
wind carried the faint stir of hoofs and a sound of voices. "Damn
the Army," he muttered. "Those rifles could easily have been set
down in Cheyenne." Except for the Army, they would not have
been under a responsibility to take on a patrol of buck Indians
to recover a wagonload of destruction. Their responsibility was
to themselves and every other man who lived north of Cheyenne.
The tribe that got hold of a hundred breech-loading Springfield
rifles could clean out every ranch and trading post on the Bozeman. He stood close to Silvertooth. "Give me twenty minutes.
I'll coyote around behind them. Try to belly up to where you
can see them."

"If they've tapped the whiskey," said the wagon master, "we
can save our shells and tromp them out. Shoot, maybe they
ain't figured out how them guns work, anyhow."

Cary walked north a quarter mile to the tracks. He cut west to the coulée and crossed on the trestle. Standing there, he searched the coulée but found no pickets. He moved on. A night hawk swooped low with a stiff rush of feathers. On a far ridge, a coyote yelped. He turned his head to seek the outlines of the ponies. Finding them, he went on more cautiously, leaving the trestle and pacing carefully through the brush.

He was within a hundred feet of the ponies when he saw the Indian sitting cross-legged on the ground, holding the reins. He sank down in a reaction of shock.

A full minute slid away. Cary knew that he was as visible to the Indian as the Indian was to him, but the sentry was watching what went on in the deep brush-choked coulée. He was a young brave with a prairie cock tail on his head. A dog-skin quiver rode his shoulders. Cary read these signs and the clue of the pale bull hide hanging on the horses, and they told him Sioux, a little gang of green Ogallala warriors out hunting lonely stage tenders to murder or supernatural buffalo to kill, feats to make men of them in the lodges.

As he rose, he winced at the leathery *creaking* of his boots. He made out a sound of stone on wood, a deep-throated voice raised briefly in a laugh. The warrior rocked forward to look into the wash.

Sam raised his arm high in a signal. He breathed deeply, flexing his arms to ease the tautness out of them. He held the carbine lightly and began moving up behind the horses.

Now he could glimpse the action in the coulée through the tumble of boulders and brush on the stony slope. A tiny fire burned against the sand. Five Indians in hip-length leather shirts, breechclouts, and leggings were busy about a freight wagon. One stood in the wagon. Two others were attempting to yoke a span of oxen to the wagon. The rest were occupied in opening crates with rocks or in examining the guns. There was no sign or smell of whiskey. A young buck raised a rifle to his cheek and sighted it, the barrel lining precisely on Cary. His heart exploded in his breast. But an instant later the brave lowered the gun and shook it as if to hear it rattle.

Cary settled his feet in the gravel, his left shoulder to his target, his right elbow extended. His finger painstakingly took up trigger slack. The gun barrel lifted with a roar, the butt thrusting solidly against the packed muscles of his shoulder. He pulled the loading lever and sprinted forward. He saw the seated Indian lurch forward and sprawl out into the coulée.

The tight huddle of ponies split open like a dropped melon. Two ponies plunged into the wash. A Sioux seized the mane of one and swung himself across its back. He turned and fired a carbine at Cary as his heels hammered the horse's ribs. The shot went through the brush with a rattle of broken twigs. The brave vanished in the dark.

A man was running along the bank with a *thud* of boots. A large and reassuring shadow, John Silvertooth sprawled at the lip of the barranca and lay in the brush with only his head exposed. His gun pointed like a finger at the Indian in the wagon, who was crouched in the deep bed with a gun thrust between the sideboards.

Sprawling opposite him, Cary heard the slam of the brave's gun. Grit exploded in his face, cutting his forehead in a wide and dull pattern of pain. He fired back and saw the splintered hole where the ball went through the wagon's side. He could hear the brave moving in the wagon. Then the flash of Silvertooth's rifle illuminated the coulée and the Indian in the freight wagon moved convulsively.

Running low, an Ogallala jumped the wagon tongue, shot past the single yoke of oxen, and made for a break in the creek-bed. Cary fired. As the pouring echoes faded, he saw the brave writhing on the sand.

Somewhere, out of sight below the rim of the bank, two more coppery bodies moved, heard but unseen. Cary waited, thinking more about the man who had ridden up the wash. He lay still, alert for the tread of moccasins behind him. Then he heard a soft rush below. A hand came into sight on the rim of the wash. The Indian got his hold and vaulted up six feet in front of him, wide-stanced and stooped, a stocky warrior in a red breechclout and long shirt. He searched the darkness for an instant before discovering Cary. He held a short axe stolen from the wagon. Suddenly finding the long shape sprawled before him, he hurled himself forward.

Cary fired and rolled away. The Indian struck the ground, pinning Cary's legs. He moved spasmodically. A moment later Cary became aware that the remaining warrior had lunged up the bank below John Silvertooth, a rifle raised in his hands like a war club. Silvertooth fired once and the man turned and slid down the bank.

They lay there. There was a confused sound of oxen lunging about, chained to the wheels and unable to escape. Silvertooth's voice came: "Sam?"

"All right. You?"

"Fit. Heard anything out of that other one?"

"I'm listening."

They waited twenty minutes before they descended to the wash. The Sioux were out of action, the guns unharmed, but Cary could not relax. "I'd give half the guns to have that one back. Did you see the shields on their ponies? Those were Thunder Fighters, Esconella's blood brothers. . . ."

Silvertooth halted in the act of searching out a keg of whiskey. He straightened. "Hell!" he said.

Cary unchained the oxen. "I'm not afraid of losing their love . . . but damn it, these breech-loaders were going to be a surprise."

139

"Maybe they hadn't figured them out."

A realistic man, Cary did not answer. Silvertooth came to help him handle the oxen, and presently Sam threw off the whole notion of Indians with a shake of his head. "If we don't get back before sunup and throw this one in line with the others, you can write off the rifles anyhow."

Bill Orrum came from the hot and windy night into The Nations. The trader moved with a loose, easy slouch. He wore a leather shirt, leather breeches, and moccasins; his black pigtails were tied with greasy knots.

A crowd of railroad workers was hoorawing at the bar. Orrum found a table near a chuck-a-luck game. He bought a bottle of whiskey and poured his drink. He thought of Sam Cary. Orrum, the pigtailed, dark dweller of wilderness places, was not an overly proud man, but he knew how to bring resentment to maturity. He thought about the trip up the Bozeman Trail to the Montana mines, which was to think about Indians. For thirty years he had taken care of himself in this country. He had got along because he was like his hosts—silent, savagely practical, vigilant, not too hankering toward luxuries. Yet for the sins of other white men he must pay, also, and the price was smokeless fires and sleeping away from his camp. If trouble came, he counted on his payload to get him through. He carried a hundred and fifty ancient smooth-bore muskets the Army had abandoned in a warehouse twenty years ago. These could be sold decently in Butte—or traded for his scalp.

Darkness came and he was aware of Mark Stockwell in the doorway. Seeing him, Stockwell approached and sat at the table where Orrum drank whiskey and played solitaire, a man very much alone.

"Cary and Silvertooth just left camp," the trader said shortly. He was perspiring. A man of massive strength, he had a firm

140

and compact form; his chest was deep and his neck short. He looked to Orrum like a man it would he easier to kill than to hurt, insulated from injury by the slow and easy power of his body.

"Watching Cary middling close, ain't you?" Orrum remarked.

Stockwell's eyes were sourly displeased. "You didn't sell him the guns?"

Orrum poured again from the bottle. "He raised the money. I hadn't got any choice."

Stockwell pressed the heel of his fist against the table with slow and bitter force. "Damn it, I'd have given fifty dollars apiece for those rifles. Why didn't you come to me first?"

"I didn't go to him. Cary came to me, six months ago, as soon as the Army said no guns. I tried to save them for you. When are you putting out?"

"Can't say. Before Cary, I hope. You'll go back to Independence?"

Orrum turned a green glass ring on his finger. "Montana."

Stockwell's thick brows raised. "Up the Bozeman?"

"How else?"

"What for? You're traded out, aren't you?"

Orrum's eyes had a spark of humor. "You're full of wonders about other people's business tonight."

Stockwell had a tenacious and unhumorous mind. He turned to signal a bartender and again stared into the shiny, taut-skinned features. "You may as well travel with me. You'd better travel with some train."

"I figure I'm better off alone than with somebody the Sioux don't like."

"Such as me?"

"You and the younger set get along. The whiskey drinkers. The warrior societies. I've heard you and Esconella meet behind the barn and smoke the pipe together."

Temper stiffened Stockwell's lips. "Is that what you hear?"

"I hear it direct," said Orrum. "I wouldn't trust him too far, you know. Esconella may be a chief's son-in-law, and the old man may be paralyzed, but . . . I wouldn't trust any of them. The purtiest sight in the world is an Injun's back . . . in your rifle sights."

"I don't worry about the Sioux. I'm north of their grounds. But it pays to keep right with all of them. What are you taking along?"

"Trade goods."

"Beads and tobacco, eh . . . and a bunch of guns?"

"A few old cannons the Army gave up long ago."

"Trade guns," Stockwell said.

"Why, Mark," Orrum said, "trade guns for Injuns?"

Stockwell grunted, seeming offended that the idea had been given words. "Don't be a damned fool. I live up there, too, you know. I don't want guns in their hands any more than Cary."

"Of course the Sioux don't range about your post, though, if you wanted to get rid of some betwixt here and Cary's place. They've got gold these days, since they learned what it was for and Wells, Fargo put it in their way."

Stockwell's first reaction was a slowness to grasp it. Then his brows pulled in and he said softly: "You've rubbed up against too many of them. You've taken their ways."

Orrum said: "This is their country, Mark. You take their ways if you want to get along. And you ain't going to get along whilst Cary's splitting the business with you."

"I can get along without putting guns in their hands."

"If Cary don't shut you out first. The Army will be back. Maybe not this year, likely next. He's a sharp trader, Mark. When the travel is going up the Bozeman instead of short-cutting him by going around, why, you'll see what I mean. You had a year of bucking him before the Army ducked out, didn't you? Kind of slim tradin', I'll reckon."

A smoke of resentment fumed in Stockwell's eyes, as though he were angry at the trader for having brought up something that was better left alone. He finished his whiskey and stood up. "I'll be leaving tomorrow night. Meet us up the line if you want to go along."

"Thanks," Orrum said.

Cary awoke at sunup, when the bugles at Fort Russell began sounding their mixed glee of brassy calls. He heard his bull-whackers turning out. Ironware *clanged* and burning mesquite roots sent their smoky incense about the corral. Lost sleep and reaction from the night's activity dulled him.

Quitting his blankets, which lay under a wagon, he stood in the harsh sunlight and pulled on his shirt. The arms wagon occupied its place in the hollow square of freight wagons. Neither the first nor the last, it was merely another great-wheeled Murphy with its tongue run up under the wagon ahead. They had completed the drive from Sweetwater Coulée two hours before sunrise.

Cary somberly regarded the stork-like tank by the tracks, slowly dripping water into the salt-crusted puddle beneath it. He resented the trash about camp and the shirtless men yawning their way through pre-breakfast chores. This, thank God, was their last day in Cheyenne.

Today Gaybird Phillips came. There would be the difficulty of explaining to her why she must not make the trip to the border this summer. There would be the task of getting her back on a train tomorrow. And then everything would simplify, and he could slot his problems plainly enough—yoke the oxen and turn them north.

As he ate, he took notice of a buoyancy among the men. They were all as sick of the camp as he was. They looked forward to the trail, with all its dangers. Breakfast over, he gave the order to slip the wheels and tar every axle. Before the job was finished, the men were glancing up the tracks, anticipating the arrival of the passenger train. Work trains hammered through from the supply depot, heading west.

A little after noon, the telegrapher's key *rattled* in the small yellow station with its two mud chimneys. The stationmaster came from the door to flap a sheet of paper.

"She comes! Forty-five minutes."

Cary killed some more time, his mind trying phrase after phrase. How to tell the girl without hurting her feelings? But better a hurt feeling than a lost scalp.

He started to move to the station to await the train, and then something caused him to glance at the loading dock across from the yellow railroad shack. In the bleached yellow sunlight, Donovan's barrels still stood awaiting removal. Silvertooth had come up beside him. Cary was conscious of his testy gaze as he, too, regarded the barrels. Cary removed his Stetson and sliced perspiration from his forehead with his finger, and then replaced the hat, and said: "I reckon Donovan's forgotten those barrels."

They crossed the corral and stood by the rear of Donovan's lead wagon. The two trailers were packed, but the gate of the main wagon was down and from the half packed interior drifted a vapor of tobacco. Cary looked at the big man sprawling against a stanchion. Suddenly discovering him, Donovan casually swung his legs overside. He regarded Cary with a shallow mask of respect. "You've got four barrels on the dock," Cary said.

"Sure, no one told me," said Donovan blandly.

"Someone's told you now. Silvertooth will help you move them. Unpack them all and repack the goods in the wagon."

The Irishman tucked a thumb under his belt. "I've heard it said Mark Stockwell is the best freighter in Wyoming. He carries his goods in the barrels they come in. Why can't you?"

"I'm not selling barrels. Why should I carry them?"

Donovan frowned, but after a moment, his hazel eyes not leaving Cary's face, he began to smile craftily, and from his pocket he brought a small handful of coins. He glanced down at them. There was still the fifty-cent piece Silvertooth had loaned him, but there were, in addition, glints of gold. He looked beyond the men, at others of the bullwhackers who were within earshot. His expression subtly changed.

"Mister Cary," he said in bluff and artificial good-nature, "you can do what you damned please with your barrels. I'm quitting."

"You can't quit," Silvertooth snapped. "You're into us for sixty dollars."

Donovan turned Cary's palm up and triumphantly dropped six gold pieces upon it. "I got onto that a week ago. You wouldn't Shanghai a man, but you'd let him drink himself into your debt before he found out what kind of a circus he was into. I say this evens us up. I talked with Mark Stockwell on the way back. He advanced me the money to pay you off. I'm going to Montana with him."

Cary tossed the coins in his hand in mild wonder. He looked up at Donovan and saw him braced for trouble. He chuckled and set the coins on the wagon bed. "You're a quick-headed mick. Only you can't buy out of my army, the way you did Uncle Sam's."

"Can't I?" said Donovan. "I reckoned I already had."

Cary's eyes ran over him, as they had that first day the Irishman came looking for work, hunting flaws and not finding any. His shoulders were sloping and massive, blotched with large freckles. The smell of him was of whiskey gone sour and sweat upon sweat. He was a testy and tough man, something for the wilderness to bruise its knuckles on. Donovan's eyes doggedly met his for a moment, and then slid down to a point on Cary's buckskin shirt and held there.

Cary asked quietly: "What's the matter, Donovan? Do we make the coffee too strong for you?"

"No," Donovan growled. "You set a man to do a boy's chore . . . repacking a wagon that's sound as a knot. We've been ready to move for five days. But we police and cook and stand guard until a man'd think he was back in the Army. And we'll kape on doing it, until Mister Cary's young lady comes on the train. You'd let ten tons of pork rot rather than miss the chance of hauling a hundred and ten pounds of young female to your post."

Cary heard the careful silence of the camp. A man casually walked between Donovan's wagon and the next, stopping where he could watch. A muscle rippled under the smooth mahogany of Cary's jaw.

"We can leave the young lady out of it," he said mildly. "Are you afraid of the Sioux? Or of me?"

Donovan's eyes lighted. He stood before the trader, a strapping man with a splayed nose and protruding ears. He stood taller than Cary and outweighed him. Cary saw in his eyes that he had been long at the brawler's evil of comparing. Donovan's thumb gouged at the bowl of his pipe. "I don't fear the Sioux," he said, "and I ain't yet met the man I fear."

"That's fine," Cary said. "It doesn't do to fear Indians. They smell it on you, like a dog. And I like a man that will stand up to another. That's why I'm glad you're coming with us."

Donovan looked puzzled. "I told you I was going with Stockwell. I had the advance so's I could pay you off."

"Did Stockwell know how you were going to use it?"

"It's my say how I use it."

"Not when you use it to put a man in a hole. No trader worth a damn would lend you money to leave another short a hand. Nobody but a trader like Stockwell. You'll take it back to him."

Donovan grinned maliciously. "You weren't afraid of leaving the Army in a hole when you loaned me the money to buy out, were you?"

Cary's eyes puckered thoughtfully. "Maybe they knew what they were doing, at that. Maybe they'd already tagged you, the way they do a blown-out musket. I and C, eh? Inspected and Condemned. . . ."

Donovan's weight leaned forward onto his toes. He put his hand up to tap Cary's chest, but it hung there and he pointed a scarred forefinger. "I done two hitches, Cary! I seen Fetterman throw his command away to Red Cloud, and after that anything in brass made me sick. The Army never condemned me. I condemned them."

"Then you should like my army. Not an officer in the lot." His hand curled the brim of his hat. "Get onto the barrels as soon as you've returned Stockwell's money."

Donovan's boots stirred and his shoulders made a settling shrug. Cary looked into his corded red face without emotion, until Donovan's eyes moved away again, and he said: "A man might as well be in the infantry." He picked up the money, tossed it once in his hand, and sauntered off through the wagons.

"A rebel!" Silvertooth snorted. "A copper-bottomed rebel! There'll be trouble with him, I tell you."

Cary breathed deeply. "He won't make trouble. He's just letting me know that he leads better than he pushes."

Silvertooth strolled to the barrels to await the bullwhacker's return. Cary walked up the tracks, stepped onto the splintered station platform, and sat on a bench, one leg extended, the other cocked across it, letting his muscles take their ease.

He looped up as a short, toughly made man in buckskin pants and a spotted calico shirt crossed the tracks and vaulted carelessly onto the platform, recognizing Cary with a lazy hand salute. The man took a place on the bench, sopping perspiration from his forehead with a handkerchief.

"I wisht some Sioux outfit," he said, "would whoop up a rain dance and break this weather."

"Any time the Sioux break the weather for us," said Cary, "it will rain arrows."

He kept his eyes and his good-nature from Coy Mullan. Mullan was Mark Stockwell's wagon master, and that was enough. He was also a transplanted Texan who wore one pant leg in his boot and one out, and that was too much. He affected a knife in his right boot and wore a Dragoon pistol deep on his right thigh.

Mullan lighted a cigar. "I hear we've got important company coming on the train. Envoy from the Great White Father to Crazy Dog. Man named Merritt."

"God help us, then," Cary said. "We'd almost lived down the trouble the last envoy made."

"It's time for a peace talk. The Piegans raided down into the Gallatin Valley last month, before we left. If they team up with the Sioux, we're both finished."

"I thought Stockwell kept them all happy with stick candy and forty-rod whiskey?"

Mullan smiled. "He could show you some tricks, at that. He smokes the peace pipe with them with one hand and steals their buffalo robes for a dime apiece with the other."

"He'll get his scalp tanned in the bargain, one of these days."

Mullan chuckled, a calm and hard-featured man not easily aroused. He was a sort of middleman in the distaste of these traders for one for another. He grinned around his cigar. "What's the real trouble between you and Mark? You don't neither of you talk much."

"Some people claim that's a virtue."

Mullan took this impassively. He let his eyes drift off toward the wagon camp. "What's different about your outfit today?" He frowned.

Cary's eyes touched him quickly. Then he shrugged. "Maybe the trash has been picked up."

"Twenty-four wagons last night, twenty-five today. Breeding them?"

"I picked up a wagon from an emigrant outfit last night," Cary said. "They'd quit it. Oxen broke down and I bought it for the cost of the goods."

"Washtubs and churns and wimmen's fixings?" Mullan inquired.

Cary's eyes went to his face. "What are you getting at?"

"Do I have to be getting at something?" Mullan winked. "I was going to say that if you wanted to park any of your wagons in our camp today, Stockwell says it would be OK. We've already stood inspection. There's a sergeant named Casner that can smell powder and ball through six layers of duck."

"Am I carrying powder and ball?"

Mullan rose unhurriedly, pulled on the cigar, and removed it to regard the smoldering tip. "You're cagey today, Sam. But Mark and I figure we've got to lend each other a hand in this trade, if we're going to get by at all."

"Help me by keeping out of my way, then. How much was he going to charge me for this helping hand? Half the arms he thinks I'm carrying?"

Mullan looked at him and kept most of his anger out of his flat, ruddy features. "You figure you don't have much to learn about freighting, eh?"

Cary saw the raw end of Mullan's patience, and pleasantly pinked it again. "One of the first things I learned was never to trust a man who wore one britches leg in and one out."

"You go to hell!" Mullan snapped.

Cary began to chuckle. "I forgot about you Texans, Coy. Proud and sensitive as a fat Comanch' full of corn beer."

Mullan's eye flicked and his hands formed slowly into fists. Then he said brusquely: "Good luck with the Army. I hope I'm around when you take 'em on."

Cary's laughter followed him across the tracks.

Afterward Cary's face sobered. It was plain enough that Stockwell knew of the gun transaction with Bill Orrum. He was in a position to sic the Army on Cary, and, if he did not, it would not be ethics which restrained him. Cary was not sure what the commandant at Fort Russell would do if he had the report of the rifles. He was not sure what he would do himself.

Then he heard a man bawl three words: "Yonder she comes!"

III

Down the string-straight filaments of steel Cary discerned a smudge of smoke. He heard his bullwhackers running up the platform and felt the sting of Silvertooth's palm on his back. Silvertooth said as he passed: "She's eighteen now, Sam! Hard candy and pacifiers won't work no more on the lady."

The train acquired color and form and sound—a chunky little diamond stack drawing six cars, breathing dust and smoke, alkali crusting the dented boiler jacket and brass steam dome. The locomotive coasted past the station and halted, exuding heat and rusty water, a snowy feather of steam dissolving into the deep blue of the sky. From its black iron bowels escaped strange digestive noises. Trainmen dropped to the ground and a wagonload of cordwood whipped up to the tender. Passengers began to appear slowly. A conductor in a linen duster, his face bloated with heat, swung from the observation car. Mailbags were tossed to the ground.

Suddenly, down the line of coaches sitting unevenly on the tracks, through the crowd and an abrupt cloud of dirty steam, Sam saw her. Behind a bulwark of three black India rubber bags stood a winsome figure in a bottle-green gown and a white basque, a frilled parasol over her shoulder. She waved at him, but he still stood there, astonished. What had happened to her, the girl in pigtails? She was gone, and in her place stood a young woman he had never seen before. Cary went forward.

He took her hands as he reached her, smiling as she laughed up at him. "Sam, it's so wonderful!"

He felt the small fingers through the starched mesh gloves. "So a stage isn't good enough for you any more!"

She wrinkled her nose at the train, floury with alkali. "Those things! Shake you to pieces!"

"What's a Dearborn do?"

"Rocks me to sleep," she declared. ". . . Sam, about here you used to kiss me."

"Godfather's privilege?" He bent and kissed her cheek. She was a small and animated presence, bell-shaped with her full skirts and snugly fitted summer basque. He straightened, half ashamed of himself, but he found the girl in pigtails slipping away from him, taking with her his own attitude toward her. His tendency was to regard her as someone new and desirable.

Gaybird's hair was as black as ever, lustrous with brushing. In the way the gray eyes, black-lashed, looked at him there was something more personal—as though they were focused on him instead of the whole bright world.

He turned and weighed the bags. "Traveling heavier. You can thin it out tonight, unless you want me to put a couple of bulls in the traces. I took a room for you at the Rollins House."

Gaybird inspected him curiously as they moved along the platform. "Didn't you bring my wagon?"

"Sure. But the camp's pretty rough."

"I was brought up to consider hotels an affectation. We'll cancel the room." Then she caught his arm. Before the station stood an attractive red-haired girl with a dour-looking man of

151

middle age who wore a talma cape over his shoulders. "See her?"

The girl was looking at them. He saw her smile, and a moment later the red-haired girl called: "Don't forget! You're to look us up."

"The Rollins House? I won't," Gaybird promised.

Cary met the girl's eyes for a moment. They were sage-green, and not shy; neither were they bold, but with a quality of challenge in them. The man in the talma did not acknowledge them. He was absorbing the hot and dusty panorama with a stricken look.

"He's a government man," Gaybird said. "An envoy to the Indian Nations. She's pretty, isn't she?"

Cary considered. "Not to say provocative. Is the name Merritt?"

"How did you know?"

"I heard he was coming. I hope he likes it up there in the Bighorns. He doesn't look like the type who would."

They met Silvertooth. He had a hug and a kiss for her. "Hard trip, lassie?"

"Those trains!"

Silvertooth chuckled and looked the girl over. "Will she toughen up to it again, do you think?" he asked Sam.

"She hasn't decided for sure that she's going. Either way, we leave at sunup. Let the men go. Give Donovan five dollars, but don't let him out of your sight."

As they crossed the tracks, Gaybird stared archly up at him. Cary's shoulders were nervously taut under the leather shirt, but his randomly sketched face did not give him away. All his practice skirmishing was nullified by the total femininity of this girl.

They passed a coal yard. "So I haven't decided whether I'm going?" Gaybird remarked.

"Gay, we've got to talk about it."

A change came to her face, a thoughtfulness that firmed her lips. ". . . All right, Sam."

They made a perilous crossing of the street through freight outfits grinding by with the hard language of bullwhackers and the sour stench of buffalo robes. A man in a derby and striped jersey was wrestling beer barrels from a dray. He stopped to look at her; Cary was obliquely flattered. She was a dainty and memorable spectacle for Cheyenne.

They reached the hotel. He had a wish deeper than a sigh, that they might have been meeting for the first time today—that for them it did not go back to a time when she was thirteen and he was her father's partner. Spurs *jangled* on the sheet-metal floor of the dining room. At tables covered by red-and-white gingham tablecloths, train passengers were gulping down their food, alert for the train bell. Gaybird made herself comfortable before giving him her attention. She disposed of the parasol and then, linking her fingers, looked soberly at him until she laughed.

"Sam, you're so funny!"

"What do you mean . . . funny?"

"So stern. What's the matter? Are you wondering how to make me drink my milk?" Cary scratched his neck. She watched him in amusement. "And what's this about my not going up to the fort?" she demanded.

"It's the same trouble as last summer, only worse. I wrote you that the Army had pulled out. I saw the ashes of Fort Phil Kearney a week after the troopers rode out. How many immigrants and miners do you think are going up the Bozeman this year, without even the protection of a few hundred green recruits?"

She tried to be serious. "Why, I don't know, Sam. How many?"

He tapped the table. "An outfit went out last week. Those

were the first wagons this summer. They may be the last. There's a reason. The Bozeman road may be two hundred miles closer than any other route, but no road is a short cut when you die on the way."

"But we've always been friendly with the Ogallalas, haven't we?"

"With Crazy Dog's Ogallalas. He's got a crazy son-in-law named Esconella, now, who's spoiling for fight. And Crazy Dog's sick . . . sick in the legs. How big a chief is a paralyzed chief? If Esconella can tie enough yellow scalps to his lance when he goes out to proselyte warriors, then Crazy Dog is out of it. And we've got a war on our hands."

With devious feminine logic, Gaybird pointed out: "But he can't take scalps if the trail isn't being used, can he?"

Sam smiled. "No, and we can't make money. But he'd have nothing against bullwhackers' scalps, and there's a couple of trains I know of going out tomorrow."

Her chin lifted. "You're not frightening me, Sam Cary. We built the fort when the Indians were unfriendly, and we can certainly hold it against them now."

"Suppose they besiege? Fifteen hundred braves piling logs against the walls could cause a lot of damage." He saw the hurt in her eyes, and he laid his hand over hers. "I'm sorry, Gay. It's not much of a welcome home, is it? This kind of talk never built anything. But that's the situation, and I'd be second cousin to a murderer to take a woman into it. That's why I said what I did to Silvertooth. And that's why I say I want you to take the train back to Cincinnati tomorrow."

Gaybird's hand was at her throat. She pulled a thin gold chain from the bosom of her dress and showed him the wedding band laced onto it. Her face was very young and very pretty and very solemn. "I don't want to embarrass you, Sam, but . . . do you want this back? Is that what you're trying to say?"

Sam had not seen the ring since that day four years ago. He turned it briefly in his fingers. He saw that it had been engraved inside: *Sam and Gaybird, August 12, 1864.*

He looked quickly at her, but she pulled the ring away and dropped it back into her bosom. "I was a sentimental child, wasn't I? I did that after you left."

"I suppose we've got to do something about it." Cary sighed. "It's going to be awkward if somebody comes to ask me for your hand, and I have to tell them you happen to be my wife."

She laughed, but the moment was stiff. "I think we ought to remember what your father wanted for you," Sam said. "He wanted to make his stake out here and go back East. He didn't want you to have to pick a man from a couple of dozen bull-whackers and buffalo hunters. He used to talk about the streets in his home town. Shade trees, and painted houses, and galleries like the decks of a steamboat."

Her gray eyes watched his lips while he spoke. "How do you know I want those things? I've just come from white houses and shade trees. I'm dying for mountain meadows and snow creeks. They're my idea of home."

Cary frowned. "I'm the wrong man to tout the East and run down the West. But let's not forget Esconella and his Thunder Fighters. And the Sand Creek Desert."

"You forget those things when the danger is over," Gaybird stated. "But you remember the mountains."

A waiter came. He took their order and departed. They did not meet each other's eyes. Something simple, thought Cary, had been made into something complex by a mumbling parson. She was essentially someone he had never met before. Yet a backlog of memories kept him from treating her like a charming stranger.

Suddenly she asked: "Sam . . . do you think marriages are made in heaven?"

"I think this particular marriage was made in a preacher's parlor." He smiled wryly. "I remember you were so tired from the train that you almost went to sleep during the ceremony. If God entered this one in the book, he must have entered it in pencil so it could be rubbed out."

"But it was still a marriage. And we can't just ignore it. That would be sinful."

"Sin," Cary conjectured, "is for preachers." He said pointedly: "If any notion of responsibility to a certain bullwhacker who needs a haircut and a clean shirt is on your mind, forget about it."

She raised her brows. "Oh, but I don't feel obligated! Only, I think we ought to decide what we're going to do."

What needed to be done was perfectly clear, thought Cary. Yet he could not make himself use the word. He found himself hedging from his bound duty. He said: "The first thing is to settle the fort business. I'm prepared to buy you out. I wish I could give all cash, but I can't. I thought of a price of fifteen thousand for your share. I'll give you. . . ."

Her eyes fascinated him. They were gray as a winter sky, but in no way cold. They were bright and noticing and alive. They watched him hesitate over the figures.

"One thing we can agree on right now," she declared. "Indians or no Indians, I'm going back to Fort Graybull. It happens to be my home. If I'm selling my home, I want to see it again first, if only to appraise it. That's reasonable, isn't it?"

Cary leaned back, his eyes unaccountably warm. "It would seem reasonable to a woman, I expect."

Gaybird gasped in astonishment. "Why, Sam, that makes it practically an anniversary after all! It's the first time you've ever admitted I was a grown-up woman!"

In the Dearborn, closely warm and smelling of dust and creosote, Gaybird removed her basque and vest, unpinned the glistening dark couronne of her hair and stood before the mirror. Gaybird Cary—Gaybird Phillips, that was—had never looked so grown up before this mirror, she thought. She felt like a young matron visiting a niece's room. Everywhere were the tokens of girlhood, small treasures of her life in Wyoming. They seemed in surprisingly bad taste, some of them, all of them marvelously young.

Released, her hair hung in two braids coming across her shoulders. Her bosom was small but not too small. Soon her skin would darken with the stain of weather. Her eyes would appear lighter. Her lower lip was deep and rich.

Remembered impressions touched her, fragrant camp suppers in the heart of the squared wagons. A French harp singing in the prairie darkness, ungainly teamsters being awkwardly attentive. She was glad to be back.

She could hear Sam kicking up a fire and Silvertooth setting a Dutch oven and coffee pot on it. Their voices were low, but she remained quiet, and presently they forgot to be careful and she could hear them.

"Takes up where she left off, don't she?" That was Silvertooth.

"About Sand Creek, Cincinnati may begin to remember pretty fine," Sam contended.

"You couldn't talk her out of going with us?"

"She's set on it."

"Well . . . this country needs women, of course," said Silvertooth.

"You talk like a breeder," Cary told him.

"Who takes better care of his stock than a breeder? We need

157

women, and she's got her old man's toughness. No, I reckon you don't see it. You see seminary all over her. But you'll see what I mean. Heat and sand won't change her none. If she's for Wyoming, you've got a pardner for keeps." Silvertooth yawned, then: "I'll git uptown and keep an eye on the boys. A regular brawl would set us back another forty-eight hours. *'Noches.'* His boots moved off.

Gaybird smiled, poured water in a basin, and washed. Then she dressed again, left the wagon, and joined Sam for the rude camp meal.

She was washing the dishes when they heard boots stepping casually through the darkness toward them. It was Mark Stockwell. Hatless, Stockwell's crisp hair was ruddy in the light. He made Gaybird a nod and faced Cary after a moment's idle scrutiny of the camp.

"Camp looks trim. Putting out tomorrow?"

"Maybeso. You?"

Stockwell smiled. "Maybeso. I was just talking to Major Drew, at the fort, about you."

Cary stared at him. "You know we're in this together, don't you? If I get inspected, I'll see to it that every last scrap of gear you're carrying is set down."

The trader raised a glowing branch to start a cigar. "This wasn't about freight. It was about taking some passengers. This man, Merritt . . . the envoy . . . needs escort to the Bighorns. It seems Drew can't give escort, because the trail is off limits. He wanted my advice and I suggested you, your place being close to Crazy Dog's grounds."

"That's fine. Only I don't guide. Not for the Army. . . ."

"Then here's your chance to get right with the Army."

Cary picked up his coffee cup and swirled it. "What's this fellow expected to do? Arrange a treaty single-handed?"

"He's a sort of flunky to lay down the rug for the real treaty parley. He'll feel out the Ogallalas. If they're amenable, he'll arrange for a full-scale parley at Fort Laramie this fall . . . feathers and brass and medals, all the usual la-de-da."

"What's he like?"

"Cold as yesterday's dishwater. His wife's a beauty. Too bad she isn't the envoy. She could pacify me, I'll bet. They're waiting in the major's office right now. I said I'd send you up."

Cary finished the coffee. "They'll have a wait, then. I can't leave Gaybird alone."

"That's the part of this mission I like best." Stockwell smiled. "I'll take charge of Miss Phillips until you come back. I'd like her opinion of some dress goods I'm taking up, anyway. If she likes it, there's a bolt for her."

Annoyance shaded Cary's face, but Gaybird spoke quickly: "Sam, you must! Could anyone guide him better than you?"

Cary sighed, and pulled his hat from the bag where it rested. "Nobody could guide him more reluctantly. All that will come of it is slow travel, and sunburn for Merritt. The Army will nullify whatever he accomplishes. But I'll talk to them."

In the silent blackness before dawn, the Fort Graybull outfit broke camp. With a grind of tires rocking across the railroad tracks, the wagons pulled into the long column. The sounds were heavy and muffled, of oxen lunging along with gaunt heads swinging, of spokes and axles mumbling to themselves in the roil of white night dust. A few miles ahead moved the gray ghost of Mark Stockwell's train. Stockwell had broken camp just far enough ahead of Cary to get the lead, with its advantages of clean water holes and fresh graze.

At Fort Russell, Cary rode inside to pick up the Army ambulance that would carry the Indian envoy and his wife. The commandant, and Cary's own good sense, had prevailed over his prejudice. Better to work with the Army than against it. He would provide escort to Dr. Merritt.

In a week, Cary made Fort Laramie and quitted it. North of Cheyenne, Laramie was sanctuary. Beyond Laramie, security was a man's own problem. The nearest walls, beyond burned ones, were at Fort Graybull, on the border, two hundred miles away.

Moving deeper into Indian country, a primitive sort of dispatch governed each action and back of this tautness of order marched the shadow that was its cause. Short of ruined Fort Reno, on the Dry Fork of Powder River, Cary caught sight of the Montana wagons on a ridge a few miles ahead. During the noon layover, Stockwell came loping back with Coy Mullan. He pulled in beside Cary to hand him a shard of pottery.

Cary frowned and turned it over. "Where'd you find it?"

"Inside the fort. There's the rubbish of a big camp."

"How many bucks?"

"I make it a hundred and fifty," Mullan said.

Cary tossed the pottery aside. "What do you want to do about it?"

"Team up. We've got to . . . for security. Fifty wagons are better medicine than twenty-five."

Cary shrugged. "I'd rather know where my enemies are than have to guess at it."

The muscles of Stockwell's jaws creased. "Have your joke. But you've got women to think of. I'll hold off squaring up tonight until you let me know."

Cary did have women to think of. He knew that, and it was the only thing that could have made him travel double with Mark Stockwell. He said: "All right . . . for the women. But we'll travel wagon and wagon, and the security plan will be mine."

Stockwell nodded briefly. He rode back to his train.

Breaking out of the layover, Cary helped Dr. Merritt hitch

his mules. Then he mounted his own pony and held it by the forewheels of the ambulance.

"Easier traveling from here on." He smiled. "We hit Fort Reno tonight. We'll join up with Stockwell, for less dust and more security. Then we head up into God's country . . . where there's water for shaving again."

"I'll believe there's water when I see it," Merritt replied grimly.

"And when we see it"—Dale Merritt, his wife, smiled—"we won't recognize it for mud."

"You'll recognize this," Cary promised.

Merritt tooled the team along through the rising dust. "Sometime you might give me a tip on how to get around these head-hunters I'm to parley with. They say there's a way to make a fool of any man."

"I wouldn't recommend making a fool of these people," Cary said. "Not of Crazy Dog. He may be old and half crippled, but he's still the big chief. He's got a son-in-law, Esconella, who'd like to depose him, but you'll still deal with Crazy Dog, and he's as sharp as a skinning knife. Put yourself in his place. He's got his back to the wall, and now we're trying to take away the wall."

"If I'm not being inquisitive," Merritt asked dryly, "whose side are you on?"

"Until the arrows begin to fly, I'm on theirs. I'm for trying to buy trail rights from them, not steal them." He felt his patience thinning for this dour man who could not understand that in the country of the red man, the white man was alien.

Dale Merritt was drawing something from a knitting bag on her lap. She was a small-waisted, red-haired girl with eyes that were actually green—glass-green—and Sam Cary remembered things he had heard about green-eyed women.

"Will you give another greenhorn some advice?" She tossed

him a slightly wilted prairie blossom. "I want to know if that's what you call kinnikinnick."

Cary studied it in mock seriousness. "Not quite. Kinnikinnick is a mess of bark, leaves, and dirt the Indians smoke instead of tobacco. So do I, when I can't get tobacco."

Dale laughed. "Asa, I've made a fool of myself. You see," she told Sam, "I botanize . . . collect flowers. Sometimes I press them. Usually I paint them in watercolors. It's quite fashionable in the East. I'd be the talk of Washington if I could go back with a collection of genuine Wyoming wildflowers. Would you have time before it's dark tonight to point out some plants to me?"

Cary glanced quickly at the doctor, who regarded his wife in slow gravity and then gave his attention again to the laboring mules. Cary hedged. "After the chores, if there's time. Doctor, I could show you some herbs that would match anything in your bag."

Merritt grunted. "For suddenness, perhaps. No, thanks."

Dale's eyes veiled themselves momentarily as Cary looked doubtfully at her, and she smiled. "After the chores, then."

In mid-afternoon they reached the shell of Fort Reno, on the Dry Fork of Powder River. The gap-toothed picket walls and burned structures loomed on a sagebrush bench above the river. The sun struck brassily on aisles of muddy water between sandbars. Where the land had not been cleared, sage and lean cottonwoods fringed the river.

Cary corralled the wagons with Stockwell's on the flat ground between the old stables and the fort proper. He sent the stock to the river to be watered.

Day scouts ranged in and four horsemen rode out. At the wooden dishpan, Gaybird finished her dishes. She wore a striped dress that Sam had told her made her look like candy; it was roman-striped, full below, snug above. Wind and heat had richened her skin; her eyes were a lighter gray, her lashes darker.

Cary had been absent from their mess, but now he came up from the *bosque*.

". . . I'll borrow your buggy rifle for Missus Merritt," he said.

"What in heaven's name for?"

"Precaution. She's got it in her head to collect wildflowers."

"Why, that's ridiculous! You wouldn't dare go far enough to find anything the stock hadn't trampled. She can find her flowers right in the corral." Gaybird's cheeks heated.

"I don't mean to get out of sight." Sam shrugged.

"I'd rather you left the rifle," Gaybird said. "The idea in giving it to me was for protection, wasn't it?" Her cheeks were flushed.

"That's right. And I'll bet, if you had to, you couldn't break a vinegar jug at ten feet!"

Gaybird's chin tilted. But she was suddenly unsure what her voice might do, and she turned her back on him.

Sam laughed and strode off.

Dale was waiting when he arrived at the ambulance. The doctor was off at his evening chores, pulling aching teeth and puncturing boils.

They moved down the meager slope to the stream. A scout loafed out westward, the tail of his pony streaming. A shoulder of cottonweeds bent the stream. They rounded it and Cary halted to pick a blossom.

"Evening Star," he said. "Scarce, down here."

She turned it in her fingers. "Then I may as well start with it. I like things that are scarce."

"Missus Merritt," Sam said, "you talk like a prophet sometimes. In parables."

"That's almost the only way a woman can talk, isn't it?"

He dipped a cup of water for her colors and gathered a small bunch of flowers. She began to sketch. Cary sat against a rock to smoke. He was impressed with the strangeness of her being the wife of a dry-minded man like Merritt.

"Do you like being a trader, Sam?" she asked suddenly.

"If I didn't, I wouldn't be one."

"Still, you'll have to admit there are disadvantages to your life."

"Just one," Cary declared. "Sometimes I have to go into town."

"One thing you must miss. Women."

He shrugged. "Something else you can get used to doing without, like whiskey."

"Tell me something," Dale said. "Are you in love with Gaybird?"

Cary looked into his pipe. "She's just a child, isn't she?"

"A beautiful and mischievous child. I think she's playing you against Mark Stockwell."

"Gaybird happens to be my partner, not my fiancée."

"I don't meant to intrude in anything you don't want me to," Dale said. "We'll talk about something else, if you'd rather. We'll talk about how wrong women can be. I was wrong about being a country doctor's wife. It looked dramatic, to a girl who didn't like being a grocer's daughter. But there's less drama to it than there is penny pinching. Then I was wrong about being a diplomat's wife. I made Asa take this political job, through a friend who went to Washington. But we landed in a Mexican desert town, instead of in Paris. And now we're in the middle of nowhere. In fact, this is the closest thing to excitement I've had yet."

"I'd say we'd had more dust than excitement."

"Does excitement always have to mean Indians?"

"Missus Merritt"—Cary sighed—"you're talking in parables again."

Smiling, she looked down at her sketch. "This is really one of the nicest specimens of wildlife I've done."

It was not professional work, but it was skilled amateur. The colors were deep brown, rose and white against the green of mountain ash. The face was his own—long, hard-fleshed, dark. He took it from her, thinking sadly of that somnolent man who was her husband. He slowly tore the page twice, dropping it on the ground.

"That wasn't very mannerly, Sam," Dale said crisply. "What did you think I meant by it?"

"I don't know. I can guess what the doctor would think."

Suddenly a change entered her face, a rush of apprehension. Cary heard the slow tread of boots. The lean form of the doctor came into view. Dale picked up the stool quickly and started toward him. Cary followed her.

"Find what you wanted?" Merritt asked.

"I made a wretched job of it." Dale shrugged. "Coming back with me?"

"No. I'll stretch my legs a bit."

"Better make it quick," Cary advised him.

Dale took her husband's arm. "Sam's right, Asa. Don't worry me by wandering about."

Merritt patted her hand. "Never worry over any man." He smiled. "It puts lines in a woman's face. And then . . . who knows? . . . perhaps she can't get another."

Dale said—"Do hurry, then."—and walked on.

Merritt watched them, his wife and the trader, a slender feminine form and a lanky masculine shape. *Twenty years ago,* he thought, *I'd have outweighed him.* But this was not twenty years ago. This was tonight, and Dale's eyes were so guileless he was certain they hid a deeper guile than any she had yet shown him. He proceeded to the point where the rumpled earth showed him they had stopped.

He was ashamed of his suspicions, but he could not take his

eyes from the ground. He saw where she had sat, the feet of the camp stool plainly in the ground. He found, by heel marks and a small rubble of burned tobacco, where Cary had sat. Then he saw the torn sheet of drawing paper. Curious, he picked it up. It was no trouble to fit the pieces together. He regarded Cary's features without changing expression. His hands slowly made a packet of the drawing paper and he slipped it into his pocket.

He stood that way, his eyes lost in bitter reverie, until a falling pebble startled him. He faced around, half frightened, his head full of the Indian tales the bullwhackers told one another. A whistler squirrel popped into a hole.

His face somber, he started slowly back to the wagon camp.

IV

Out of the badlands a wind came to hiss over the rabbitbrush and whip hot sand through the wagons. For two days the wagons groaned across the hot current of it. One morning they discovered the ghost-like outline of the Bighorns to the northwest. At Crazy Woman's Fork of the Powder they lumbered through a wide alley of alkali water and sandbars. In two days they would make the transition from desert to pines.

By process of rotation, Bill Orrum had worked up to the head of the wagon train. He would have felt safer traveling with a riding mule and a pack animal than in this lumbering company of bullwhackers. His only compulsion was to sell the wagonload of ancient smooth-bore muskets he carried, and he began to be impatient to make a deal short of Montana. The rifles weighted him like an anchor, but Stockwell was still evasive about closing with him.

It seemed timely that the trader should jog by the wagon this mid-afternoon with his hat tugged down against the cold north wind and his carbine slanted across his saddle. Stockwell's eyes were on the foothills ten miles west. He was staring attentively when the gunrunner said: "Got a minute, Mark?"

Stockwell looked around. "No more than that. There's a herd of antelope over yonder. I'm one trader that's had a bellyful of jerky."

The mules humping up a long slope, Orrum struck a match for his pipe. "I wouldn't rush into a hunt in these hills, Mark. You rushed into trading about the same way, though, didn't you?"

"No. Who told you I did?"

"A man that braces an old-timer like Cary is either a greenhorn or an optimist."

"I thought I'd done pretty well. The cash book's fat enough."

Orrum saw ill-nature darkening Stockwell's face. "You know how it seems to me? Merritt's the man you want to worry about. Not Cary."

"How's that?"

"You get fat on trouble, Mark. Cary gets fat on peace. Merritt's a peacemaker."

A hard smile shaped Stockwell's mouth. "What kind of a peacemaker?"

"He's got a good teacher. Cary aims to help him make a treaty, too. Then where'll you be?"

Stockwell said: "I don't think I've got much to worry about. Esconella's promised scalps and powder to half the tribes in Wyoming. Crazy Dog is finished as a chief."

"Be a good idea to know how you stand with Esconella, anyhow. There ain't nothing that tickles an Injun like a new rifle. And them rebel Sioux are going to need guns if they tackle a log-walled post. I could be talked out of these I'm carrying, I reckon."

Orrum saw the same expression in Mark Stockwell's eyes that he had seen in Cary's the day he paid him for the guns. He wondered what made a man think he was any better than the men he traded with.

"It hasn't come to that yet, and I hope it won't."

He swung his horse away, but heard Orrum remark: "From now until we hit Fort Graybull, there'll be Injun eyes on us every hour of the day. There was fifteen hundred that cleaned out Fetterman. I wonder how many'll hit us? If you want to make a trade with them, Mark, make it soon."

The wind wrestled with the wagons as they sidled from the backbone of the ridge into the *bosque* of a creek. Cary shouted them into formation on the streambank. While he was finishing this chore, he saw Mark Stockwell riding in; he had not seen Stockwell since he took off three hours earlier to hunt antelope. It was a few minutes later that Silvertooth came after him. The wagon master's sand-scoured face was lined.

"Come over here," Silvertooth said shortly.

Stockwell stood with a half dozen bullwhackers and Coy Mullan in the lee of a freight trailer. Conversation halted as the men approached.

Silvertooth, breathing deeply, said: "Tell him about your Injun, Stockwell."

Something in Cary tightened.

His face ruddy, Stockwell said: "I had to kill an Indian out there. We nearly bumped into each other, hunting. I happened to drop him first."

Cary swung at the trader's head. Stockwell went down among the boots of the teamsters, Cary lunging after him. But Silvertooth was there to pin Cary against a wagon, and suddenly bullwhackers were piling onto both men to separate them.

The blood slowly left Cary's head. He said: "So you killed a buck. We were within aces of making a treaty to open this country up again. And you had to kill a Sioux."

"It's always open season on us," Stockwell snapped, "but I

have to let them take first crack at me . . . is that it?"

"He was hunting antelope, not traders, or he wouldn't have been alone."

Silvertooth growled: "Well, it's done. We'll know in a day or two how much harm's been done. Where'd you leave him?"

"In a wash."

After a moment Cary said: "Donovan, go get Doctor Merritt. It's time Stockwell and I had a talk with him."

Donovan returned with the envoy. The doctor's face was raw with sanding, his eyes black and dull as nail heads. He demanded: "What's more important than my finishing my supper in peace, Cary?"

"Finishing the trip in peace. You wanted to meet Crazy Dog? Well, you're about to have the opportunity. We're leaving for the village tomorrow."

Cary waited for his dignified hedging, while Silvertooth swore under his breath and the other men stirred in surprise. But after a moment's thought the doctor said: "You mean we'd go up alone, without escort?"

"It doesn't take a troop of cavalry to carry an olive branch."

The envoy's dark eyes crinkled. "Well, why not? The kill or cure treatment for Indian troubles, eh? I'll be ready."

Cary turned to Stockwell. "In the meantime, you can make up a pack load of trade goods. Don't skimp. I'll present them to Crazy Dog and tell him about your buck before he catches his breath. It's the only way I know of to handle it. You might throw in that ring you're wearing, as a token of mourning. . . ."

An hour after sunup, Cary, Dr. Merritt, and Donovan left the train. Silvertooth put the wagons back on the road for the fort. Whips and leather lungs snapped the line into shape, scouts ranged distantly, and the dogged monotony of the trail settled again as chokingly as the dust.

Bill Orrum tooled his wagons into the train. He was in the cloud of earthy smoke at the rear when Mark Stockwell pulled in beside him. Stockwell handled his horse cavalierly. Of his features, masked against the dust, only his eyes were revealed.

"Still think you'll try it alone, eh?" Stockwell inquired.

"Bound to. I aim to drop out of the train. I know a short cut through the foothills. I'll be in Butte before you're at Fort Stockwell. I'd like to be heeled when I get there, too. These customers of mine, now, don't always pay in cash money."

Stockwell put a slip of paper into the gunrunner's hand. "Give that to my manager at the fort."

Orrum tucked it into the sweatband of his hat. "Thanks, Mark. May seem steep, but think of the risks."

"You're right it's steep. Smooth-bore muskets for the price of Spencers! That's Cherry Spring, now? Don't be in any rush to close in with Esconella. I'd like to clear Fort Graybull and be heading up into my own country before the bucks get the guns out of the grease. Stall them for a while, if you can. This is close timing."

They gripped hands briefly. Orrum pulled his wagon and trailer out of line and pointed it northwest.

That night, with twelve miles behind them, Cary camped on a green meadow under fragrant pines. In the morning, he and Donovan talked it over.

"We should make the village before night, if they haven't moved," Cary declared. "As an infantryman, what's your opinion of how we should proceed?"

"Backward," said Donovan. "At least, I'm with the men this time. Did you need somebody to wash the pots?"

"If you've been bragging about the kind of soldiering you did," said Cary, "I'll take your scalp myself."

They penetrated a flinty highland of sparse timber and

bleached grasses. A buzzard tilted overhead. On a cold rim of granite, Donovan put his pony across the ridge to protect their flank. Cary loafed along the trail.

Presently Merritt called: "Will you stop at the next stream? I'm dry."

Cary swung down at a spring branch and let his horse drink. He stretched, looked about him, and knelt to scoop water in the brim of his hat. The doctor dismounted. When Cary looked up, hat brim to his lips, he saw Merritt standing there silently with a pistol in his hand. The gun was directed at Cary's belly.

Cary let the water spill. "What's this?"

"This," said Merritt, "is the wages of sin. Was she worth it, Cary?"

The pure logic of it overwhelmed Cary. Merritt, contradicting everything he knew about the man, to endorse this sortie!

"Was she worth it?" Cary repeated. "I wouldn't know. I just wouldn't know." He began to rise, but Merritt snapped, "You'd better stay down."

"On my knees?"

The doctor was all resolution and suppressed fury, which he seemed trying to liberate. "Would you like to tell me about the night at Fort Reno?"

Cary shrugged. "I didn't know she was painting my picture, Merritt. But if she was painting, she didn't have time to get into any other mischief, did she?"

"You were gone close to an hour." His hand trembled. "I don't like this any better than you do. A doctor gets used to trying to save lives. But I'm a man first and a doctor afterward."

"From what I've seen of doctors, I'd rather have one operate on me with a Colt."

"If you're going to die protecting the lady's name, then. . . ."

"This is a damned shame." Cary sighed. "It's a shame for the white traders and the Sioux. There's nothing between them and war now. And it's a shame for you, because you won't get back. And"—he sighed again—"I'm sorry for my wife, too."

"Your wife?"

"Gaybird. We've been married for four years. It was a sort of guardianship, after her father died. But it's been . . . well, subject to annulment, up to now. I was thinking it wouldn't be, by fall."

Merritt's fault, as a killer, was that he was amenable to logic. Sam saw him flashing back over the whole month on the trail. "She wears no ring," he stated.

"It wasn't meant to be a marriage. But the fact is . . . dammit," he said, "it's none of your business what's between us."

Merritt took a long, steadying breath. "It might be."

Cary peered into the intent features. "I think she thought she loved me. But that was in Cheyenne, and I still figured she was a kid, and felt obligated to me."

"I thought I detected a certain amount of affection between you," Merritt observed.

Cary wagged his head. "Of all the men to confuse affection and love, Doctor, you ought to be the last."

"Where does one begin and the other end?" Merritt scoffed.

"They're two different things. I think when Dale married you she had affection for you. But she happened to be in love with you, too, and now that the affection is gone, all that's left is love."

Merritt's bitter smile came. "How did you arrive at the conclusion that my wife had anything but contempt for me?"

"No one," Cary said, "will ever have contempt for you. People may hate you, but you've got a sort of bedside manner that lets you take over in a situation. Yet you've kept Dale at arm's length so long that her eyes have begun to stray."

"Will you give me one inkling of her love for me?" Merritt challenged.

"Sure. The fact that she's in Wyoming. She knew it was

dangerous, and yet she came with you. If she'd wanted to play it fast and loose, she'd have stayed in Washington."

Merritt's face weighed it. It silenced him.

"People ought to stick to what they're good at," Cary said. "You were a good doctor. But you threw it up to be a second-rate politician. And now that you're in a bind, do you know the one thing that's apt to get you out? Medicine. You're going to work on old Crazy Dog."

Merritt shuddered. "Man, there are seven thousand things that can cause paralysis of the limbs. One or two of them are susceptible to treatment."

"But this was the result of a gunshot. I thought maybe . . . well, it's a chance."

"You thought maybe I was God," Merritt grunted.

"I had a doctor staying at the post one winter," Cary said. "He worked on dozens of Indians. If there's a living god to them, it's a man with a brown cowhide bag. Put yourself in Crazy Dog's place. A man comes all the way from Washington, not to make a treaty, but to make him well. The white man's medicine brings the chief some relief. Maybe it cures him. Then, Doctor, he begins talking peace terms."

There was a loosening look about Merritt.

"Women are pretty strong medicine themselves." Cary smiled. "You need to be your own man when you go to dickering with them. That's been your mistake. Dale let you doubt yourself. Don't. Not for any woman."

The gun dangled in the physician's hand. He said: "And I had to travel two thousand miles to find a man who talked this good sense. Do I go back in irons, or do we go on?"

"We go on." Cary watched him turn away to pick up the reins of his horse, and he took the drink he had spilled before, and then walked to his own pony. He took a moment, before mounting, to wipe his palms carefully on his buckskin thighs.

The perspiration made dark prints on the smoked leather.

The climb stiffened. There became increasing evidence that they were in someone's dooryard—someone who left shards of old pottery about, bright scatters of arrow chips, bleached bones of buffalo. And now a horse *clattered* on the ridge, and a rider let his horse tumble down the slope. Donovan was plunging in with his tough features ropy with fear.

"In that tamarack, Cary! A platoon of the varmints, ahossback and waiting!"

Cary squinted at the dark green cones of timber masking the mouth of a cañon that funneled in between two hills. "All right," he said. "That's what we've been waiting for, isn't it?" He lifted his right hand and jogged toward the trees.

There was a flutter of color and something arched from the trees. It spun and twisted in the cold mountain sunlight and struck the ground ahead of Cary. The feathered arrow shaft slowly fell over. Cary halted, his belly muscles wadding. Everything had been a prelude to this instant, and now no man knew how the next few moments would go.

From the trees the Indians began to file, Sioux soldiers, toughened and tamed by experience. Cary looked for Crazy Dog. The chief was not in the party, but Cary saw his son, Yellow Horn.

The Sioux drew up, robed and belted, bright with ornament. Cary raised his hand again.

"How is my friend, Yellow Horn?" he greeted in Ogallala.

The Ogallala studied him. "How is it that you come?"

"The grandfather sends us. We come as an old friend and as a new one."

"What does the grandfather wish? More buffalo to steal?"

The Sioux ringed them tightly. A brave thumped the rawhide *aparejo* straddling the pack horse that carried food and gifts.

"We bring presents," Cary declared. "We bring the greatest medicine man the white man knows."

They stared at Donovan and then came close to Merritt, gaping and pulling at his brown cowhide bag. He flinched but Cary said casually: "Easy."

After a moment Yellow Horn said: "Can he cure sick legs?"

"Maybeso Crazy Dog walks again."

Yellow Horn nodded slowly. "You come," he said.

Beyond the trees a trail lifted them to a hillside that sloughed off into a wide valley. Smoke rose lazily from many fires. It was like entering a vast and untidy fairground, only instead of tents there were hundreds of teepees scattered randomly. Dogs nosed about, yapping at them. Babies squalled and squaws gathered in groups and screeched at naked boys to keep back from the Long Knives. Hides were pegged on the ground under stirring mantles of flies. Yellow Horn stopped once and pointed at a fat white mongrel dog, and a squaw laid hold of it swiftly and struck it on the head with a rock. She dragged it, twitching, away to a fire. Merritt's face sickened. "Are we . . . expected to eat . . . ?"

Cary grinned. "Best sign in the world. A dog feast."

Before a lodge where a bull-hide shield hung on a tripod, Yellow Horse slipped from his pony. He ducked inside, and presently came back to summon two warriors. They carried the paralyzed chief out. He wore a bronze treaty medal on a rawhide cord about his neck. Weight had sloughed off his stocky frame since Cary saw him last. A white buffalo robe was belted about his middle and his heavy, plaited braids came forward across his shoulders. His face was wrinkled bronze with glints of black Indian eyes.

Cary spoke briefly with the chief. From his pocket he took the ruby ring of Stockwell's. Sitting propped against a boulder,

Crazy Dog smiled and slipped it onto his finger.

"Long Rifle does not come to his friends often," he said.

"A trader is busy."

"Yellow Horn says the grandfather sends his medicine man to cure me."

Cary put a hand on Merritt's shoulder. "He has cured many white chiefs. Maybeso his medicine cures you."

"We will go inside."

The lodge was stifling with its rancid odors of hides and sweat and food. The chief mixed tobacco, lighted a pipe, and passed it. Between silences, there was talk. Then the elders rose again and all but Yellow Horn, another Ogallala, and the chief left the teepee.

Cary turned to the physician. "All right, Doctor. This is your big play. He's your patient."

Merritt asked the chief to have the fire built up so that he could see better. He said to Cary: "Can he tell me anything about this?"

"He was shot in a hunting accident. We'll say it was an accident. He hasn't walked since."

Merritt sighed. He helped the chief turn over on his face, and removed the belted robe. The firelight glistened on skin like discolored brown metal. He touched a large scar on the man's spine. Cary heard the doctor murmur. He bent over, his fingers prodding gently at Crazy Dog's back. He sat back.

"What is it?" Cary asked.

"I'm not sure. I would say he has either a large concretion alongside his spine, or the bullet is still there. But either way . . . I don't know."

Yellow Horn spoke to Cary. "He says the medicine men thought there was a bullet in him," Cary translated, "and they burned cow dung over the wound to drive it out. But nothing happened."

"Surprising," Merritt remarked. His face was glum in the warm firelight. He groped in his bag and dispensed sulphate of morphia. Suddenly he smiled. "Nervous?" he asked Cary.

"Passably."

"You should be."

"Why?"

"Because we're working on ten-to-one odds. But there's always that tenth chance."

Suddenly Donovan growled: "Here comes that squaw with a kettle! Have we got to eat that damned dog?"

"You'd pick a fight with a man who wouldn't drink with you, wouldn't you?"

Crazy Dog sat up again. They ate the dog stew. Accustomed to Indian delicacies, Cary was able to eat his share. Presently, as the morphine took effect, Merritt prepared to work. "I have candles here," he said. "Will you men hold them?"

The operation was brief. The chief grunted occasionally. Merritt carefully laid on a handkerchief a lead ball. He bluestoned the wound and fixed a dressing over it.

"All right," he said. "Let's take him outside."

Cary watched the warriors place the chief on the buffalo robe before the lodge. A staring pack of squaws, braves, and children had collected. They spoke in soft, low rushes. Shell ornaments rattled and moccasins whispered on the bare earth. Merritt eyed them uneasily.

"If they're waiting for a miracle," he said, "they're going to be disappointed. After three months, it's hardly to be expected that he should take up his bed and walk. It will take some time."

"How much time?"

"Days . . . weeks. I don't know. I should think, perhaps, only a few days."

"But by fall for sure?"

"In time for the treaty commission?" Merritt smiled. "Yes.

He'll walk by then, if he walks at all."

In the watchful silence, Cary brought the rawhide packs containing the gifts. On a blanket he set out dusky banks of tobacco, bolts of red cotton, papers of needles and spools of thread. He produced a large silver watch and demonstrated it. Crazy Dog put the watch under his robe, his eyes gleaming. It was when he moved to do this that Merritt spoke suddenly.

"There's our sign, Cary." In moving, the Indian had spread his legs slightly and again drawn them together. Cary had noticed this without being impressed. But now the doctor said quickly: "Ask him to bend his knees."

Cary translated. His back to the smoky boulder beside his shield rack, Crazy Dog placed his palms on the robe. His knees bent and rose four or five inches off the robe. Yellow Horn said something in a deep, excited voice. The dark eyes of the Sioux came to Merritt.

"Tell them," Merritt said, "he'll be able to walk within two weeks."

Cary let the moment stretch out, tightening, before he announced: "In the time of the full moon, your chief will walk from his lodge to the river. When leaves fall, he will lead the hunt."

There was a great noise of Indian voices, the tribe breaking. The old chief's smile squinted his face and he beckoned to the doctor. Merritt squatted beside him. Removing his necklace of bear claws, the Ogallala placed it about the doctor's neck. He spoke to Cary.

"He says you're the greatest healer the Sioux nation has ever seen." Cary grinned. "He wants you to treat all of his people who are sick. That would mean about ninety percent of them. If you were ever looking prestige in the eye, Merritt, it's right now."

Merritt looked about. Cary had the sudden fear that he would back out, that the smell and filth of the diseased would be too much for him. But a look of deep calm came to Merritt's face.

"You were right," he declared. "A man ought to stick with what he's good at. . . . Tell them to go to their lodges. I'll visit them all in turn."

Merritt started his grand tour of the lodges, and Cary eased into his own business. He sat in the stuffy deerskin lodge with the chief and his old men.

"The medicine man was from the grandfather," he told Crazy Dog. "The gifts were from the trader, Stockwell."

Quick, dark eyes were on Cary, keen as flashing knives. "Owns Lance is not our friend. Why does he send gifts?"

"Owns Lance wishes to be your friend. He sends the gifts in grief, because he killed one of your young men. It was by accident."

Crazy Dog's breath sounded lightly between his teeth. "Owns Lance does nothing by accident. We thought Loud Bear died in the big wind. Why did he kill him? Has Owns Lance a sickness?"

"He was afraid. He saw him in the wind and killed him before he thought."

"Why did he not bring the gifts himself?"

"Because he was afraid. Esconella has frightened many of the traders."

Crazy Dog shook his head. "The heart has gone bad in him. He has left the village of his fathers. He has four hundred men with him and he will find more. He has sent presents to the Brûlés and Hunkpapas. The whole village of Two Elks has gone with him."

"But Crazy Dog is still chief."

The Ogallala peered at him. "Crazy Dog is chief, as there is fire in flint. But first it must be struck. Without legs I cannot strike fire. If the white man's medicine is strong, Esconella will play with the boys again."

"If he comes back," Cary asked, "can you handle him?"

"He will not come back. He has sent my daughter back to my lodge. He has laughed at the Wind God. He is stubborn and stiff-necked. If he steals guns, he will be dangerous."

"If he does not steal guns, and the tribes do not take the warpath, will you talk peace with the white soldiers?"

The chief received it stolidly. "Why do they want to talk peace, when they will not keep peace? When they still steal?"

"They are sorry for the acts of white liars and thieves. They want to repay you for the buffalo they have slaughtered and the warriors that they have killed."

"What is it they want?" Crazy Dog asked sharply.

"They wish to man the Bozeman posts again. To police traders and travelers, as well as renegade Indians."

"Will they pay for this?"

"They will pay."

Crazy Dog spoke to one of the Indians. In the lodge there was a thin strand of conversation, a word grunted, a sign made. At last he told Cary: "We will make no promises. But we will talk when the leaves fall. If Crazy Dog is still chief of the Ogallalas."

Night came before Merritt was finished. Cary noticed that the Indians kept sentries out. Esconella had left nothing with his tribe but the fear of him. Cary, Donovan, and the doctor spread their blankets outside Crazy Dog's lodge. Silence came. Mountain cold pressed sharply upon them. Small fires puddled the dark ground, expiring into coals; dogs relinquished their yapping and the last child ceased to complain. The camp slept.

Cary lay with his fingers laced under his head. He pictured the wagons forted up tonight on the lap of Red's Meadow. At noon tomorrow they would ford Silvertip Creek, and before nightfall they would make Fort Graybull, on Young Woman Creek. Cary himself hoped to make it by dark.

From the blankets at his side, Merritt's voice came with the solemnity of a sleep-talker. "It's here, Cary. It's all right here. They sent me out to make a fool of myself. Wyoming . . . the graveyard of diplomats. But I didn't make a fool of myself. By God, I didn't!"

With a guide and a pack horse loaded with gifts, they left the village at sunup. Working down from the crests, their guide took them through a swift descent, finally pulling up on a timbered ridge above the grassy foothills. He pointed with his rifle.

"Half day ride." The gun barrel swerved southward. " 'Whackers sleepin' late!"

Cary studied a pencil of smoke rising from the hills. "No," he said. "My men would be nooning on Silvertip by now. Maybeso Esconella?"

"Esconella rides north to meet Brûlés and Hunkpapas."

"What's the varmint say?" Donovan demanded.

"He says that the smoke yonder is our camp. He says it can't be Esconella, because he's north of here, waiting for the Brûlés."

"Are they going to spoil their record about never laying siege to a fort?"

"They've never finished one."

The guide riding back, they followed a cañon onto a grassy apron. As they drew near the smoke, it became a meaningless smear, a grassy smudge against the sky. They angled up a grassy ridge, and Donovan precipitously crowded past, eager and curious. They saw him pull up on the crest, staring down. He did not turn or signal, but as they came abreast of him, they saw the burned wagons and dead bulls below them, on a spring branch called Cherry Creek.

The camp was on the bank of the creek, a trampled acre of

bruised grass and broken brush. In the center of this area of rubbish and hoof marks lay the remnants of a single wagon and trailer. The wagons had long ago burned out, but the smoke of foodstuffs and robes fumed in the wreckage. Arrows pincushioned the oxen.

They found the bullwhacker had been pinned to the ground with stakes through his wrists. Skilled, curious knives had been at his body. The corners of his mouth had been gashed and his nose was cut off. His moccasins were on his feet but his leather breeches had been cut away in several places.

How he had died, from which wound or from sheer pain, no one could have said. He was unrecognizable, but they had lived a month with that round-crowned Stetson, with the greasy buckskins and the quilled leather shirt, and they knew them instantly for trader Bill Orrum's. Nothing was missing but his black pigtails.

Everywhere lay remnants of gun chests and ammunition cases, split yellow-pine slabs stenciled in black. A few paper cartridges lay about. Using a board as a shovel, Cary scooped out a shallow grave, and Donovan dragged the gaunt body into the trench. Cary secured his clothing, dropping the Stetson with its greasy sweatband across the mutilated face, the deerskin breeches across the hips. He held the Blackfoot shirt in his hands.

Paper whispered in a pocket. Cary pulled out a fold of writing.

Mr. Williams: Please give bearer $2,000 in gold, for value received.

Stockwell

"For value received," Cary said. He and Donovan gazed at each other, and Donovan's face broke oddly.

"Damn it, Cary!" he said. "Esconella's got his guns!"

"He's got the guns," Cary said. "All he needs now is the guts."

V

Silvertooth poked along at the head of the column, slapping at flies on the neck of his mule. They were in the meadow country, at last, the green country, the country of oceans of grass and islands of pine, of water you could drink without straining and grass that didn't crackle when you walked on it.

They had spent the night in Red's Meadow, that unbelievable park just a few miles from the desert. Then they had strung out again, nooned on Silvertip Creek, and this late afternoon were working down through piney hills to the pale-green valley of Young Woman Creek, the blue-black mountains at their back.

Silvertooth, never getting far from Gaybird's wagon, carried a worry or two. Last night Mark Stockwell had pulled out with his wagons. He was taking the short cut that lopped off a few miles but denied him the comfort of a day or two in Fort Graybull before the last fifty miles of his own trip. Bill Orrum had left earlier in the day on another cut-off. Their behavior puzzled him.

From a high tuck in the hills, they had their first view of the fort. It was a half hour distant, still. Fenced by sharpened lodgepole logs, the buildings looked trim as matchboxes. Silvertooth waved the word down the line and loped out to look for his scouts. He had a treacherous desire to let down. He wanted to signal them all in: *We're done, boys, draw your pay and spend it!* But he had been through too much on the Bozeman to be fooled.

After a time he saw Tom Kane, one of the scouts, sloping in from the north. Another rider suddenly slashed up from a coulée just behind Kane, and Silvertooth's heart squeezed. But it was not a Sioux. After a brief conference, the pair came in at a hard lope. Silvertooth waited.

The man with Kane was Coy Mullan. As they reined in on the green, granite-ribboned hillside, Silvertooth saw that the wagon master's features were ashen. He rode with his revolver in his hand. He was out of breath. He waved the gun pointlessly and gasped: "Damn the varmints! Damn them!"

Silvertooth struck the gun aside. "What's the trouble now?"

Mullan stared with a sick fear. "One of the scouts flushed Esconella and a whole gad-blamed army in a coulée, waitin' for us! We've turned back. Got three, four miles, maybe, but they're ramping down on the train like the devil splitting kindling! Mark's bringing the wagons to your fort. We're a mile and a half north, in the creek bottom."

Silvertooth turned to fire a shot and bawl a warning. An outrider snapped his arm back and forth, turned, and ran his horse at the train. By standing in the stirrups, Silvertooth was able to discern a dirty-gray flow of canvas sheets in the *bosque* of Young Woman Creek. It was the Montana train, slicing back to the post. He shuddered at the thought of the gigantic log jam of wagons crowding through the sally port at once.

He groaned then, and turned, and that was when he saw three horsemen sliding down a hill a mile to the rear. But these riders came like whites, bent low across their saddle swells.

A hosanna went up from Silvertooth's lips. Sam—Sam and Donovan and the doctor. Triumphantly he bore down on the train, no longer an old woman fussing with trivialities, but feeling himself growing.

They met at the rear and Silvertooth started to pass the word.

"We saw them from the hills," Cary interrupted. "They've got the guns Orrum was carrying. Orrum's been murdered. Better cut loose the heavy wagons and bring the rest in. Merritt and I will take the women to the fort."

With an instinct for emergency, Cary had left the arms wagon only half-loaded. He whipped it out of line with its four span of strong young mules and sent it on. He drafted a hunter to take Gaybird's wagon in, and put her on his horse behind him. Her skirts billowed at either side of the horse. As they rode, he glanced back. "You don't have to squeeze the wind out of me. I won't leave you."

She squeezed harder, closing her eyes. *Never, never,* her lips said.

They came off the last hill into the wide and indolent valley of Young Woman Creek. Near the western margin of it ran the creek in its entourage of cottonwoods and silver aspen, tender with new leaves. Hunters' trails ran down to a sandy ford about a half mile from the post walls. Marks of travois scarred the meadow and hillsides, where Indian potato and wild onion had been dug. At the back of the fort rose a small hill capped by a high look-out tower. Beyond the hill was a reach of two miles of meadow, and then the hills again, stiff with timber.

They threaded the road through the trees, feeling the moist coolness of the *bosque*. Berry thickets crowded close to the road and wild hop festooned the cottonwoods. They plunged through the stream. Silver spray drenched them. Gaybird's skirts ceased to billow; they modeled her legs glisteningly.

Shading with his hand, Cary peered northwest. He made out the Montana train lunging back to the fort. Beyond, on the slope of a distant hill, he discerned a blur of moving horses.

As they left the trees, Cary's post manager, Daniel Edge, came in sight beyond the haystacks. A two hundred and fifty pound man whose body turned everything he ate into fat, Edge swung his horse in beside them.

"A hell of a homecoming!" he shouted, his brown eyes vehement.

"You know about the Sioux?"

"The look-out spotted them. He made them at seven, eight

hundred. I've got all the men on the walls."

"How many around?"

"Maybe forty."

For round numbers, Cary reckoned, a hundred inside the post if the wagons made it in, seven to eight hundred outside.

They loped past the haystacks and outer corral. They crossed the mauled ground about the main gate. A square blockhouse dominated the northwest corner of the post, matched by a similar barn-like structure on the southeast. From loopholes in the blockhouses and along the walls, men were shouting at them. The tall gate made a two-foot slot. They crowded into the narrow, walled passage, where Indians were penned for trading in uncertain times. A sentry bawled and the inner gate grudgingly opened. They entered the post.

Cary felt Gaybird's arms relax. He heard her sigh. He explained it, too—the comfort of the walls.

The great, engulfing ocean of the wilderness could not break through the slim dike of sharpened poles. This square, no larger than a town block, had a cramped-down strength of many towns. It was a strong mix of abilities, cunning, and courage. Whoever broke that dike would not only let the wilderness pour in but would release a barbarous energy on himself.

Across two-thirds of the enclosure fell the notched shadow of the forward wall. Log and rock buildings occupied the area to the right; the remaining space was an emergency corral filled with stock. Drenched and wind-blown, Gaybird held to the stirrup as Sam lowered her. Cary faced Dan Edge. "Get the women settled. Then get on the wall. If Stockwell beats me to the gate, hold him off. If the Sioux beat us both, lock the gates. We'll stand them off outside. We've all the rifles we can use, if it comes to a showdown. Trapdoor Springfields! You'll hear 'em."

Edge ducked his chin to his shoulder to wipe a droplet of sweat. Gaybird touched Sam's hand as he moved to ride out.

"Sam! I keep thinking . . . if anything should happen . . . would we have to spend eternity in a sort of purgatory?"

Cary smiled. "Gaybird"—he sighed—"I've been in purgatory. Whatever happens, one way or another, I'm coming out of it. Be a good girl and go along with Dan. Missus Merritt will join you. You can't have a light, but I reckon you can pray in the dark."

Wheels echoed hollowly in the sally port and the Merritts rattled in. Cary struck the horse with his hat and went through the gate.

Northwest, across the cropped meadow, he quietly observed Stockwell's wagons muling through the upper ford. Spray splashed silver in the sunlight. A wagon was bogged in sand and the muleskinner was wallowing ashore to catch a ride. All the commotion of a full-scale retreat was there, teamsters standing to rawhide-stumbling mules, freight sprawling out of lurching wagons, hubs grinding together as the wagons bickered for position.

Cary brought his gaze down the timbered streambed to where Silvertooth was dispatching the first of the Graybull wagons through the water. The wagon master lingered in the shallows, swinging his carbine.

Cary tried to measure the situation, but he could not reckon which train would reach the post first. A vermilion flake of color twisted in the light on a near ridge, trembling like a dead sumac leaf. He knew it for a whirled blanket, counterpart of the white soldier's trumpet. Around it swirled a wave of acorn brown, blotting the young grass. The wave widened and swept forward, punctured with glints of steel—steel that had been files and Dutch ovens until squaw cleverness fashioned lance tips from it; browned and blued steel molded in Eastern factories for savage hands to master. He sat rubbing the breech of his gun, waiting.

It grew evident that his wagons were going to have the edge at the gate. Rambling and broken, Stockwell's gaunt line straggled across the meadow. The vanguard of Silvertooth's disciplined column was already passing the haystacks. Cary took the coiled bullwhip from his pommel and moved out before the gate.

The wave of Sioux, offscrapings of four tribes, had dimension now. It was a cloud painted gorgeously with red horsehide, with gray, green, and vermilion blankets and buffalo-hide shields. A gigantic thundercloud to drench with its fury the wagons about to jam the gate of the trading post.

Cary moved forward. He and Silvertooth met briefly. "Take them in!" Cary ordered. "Straight down the line till you hit the back wall! A jam will finish us, sure as hell!"

There was a low, grinding echo of hubs from the passage as the first wagon went in. Up on the wall they were bawling encouragement. Team after team, heads low and swinging, the oxen streamed into the post.

The first of Stockwell's wagons rambled up, driven by a wild-eyed muleskinner with a tawny beard, a standing, shirtless figure hurling his whip. Cary moved into the way of the mules. "Turn them!" he shouted.

The muleskinner's wide eyes stared. He lashed the mules again.

Cary hurled the whip against a leader's neck. The cracker drew blood; the mule lumbered against its collar mate, and he gave it the whip again. The team fell away as the muleskinner shouted and jumped down.

Stockwell came loping along the line of wagons to plunge to a halt beside Cary. His face was crusted with dirt and sweat. "They're on us, man! I had to leave some of my wagons in the creek. For God's sake, keep them moving!"

"Line them up before the gate," Cary said. "They'll serve as a final firing line."

Stockwell seized his shirt front. "You aren't God Almighty! They can all go in, one and one."

Then he was looking at the paper Sam took from the bleached ribbon of his Stetson. His eyes rushed back to Cary's face, a stark questioning in them. He knew then what had happened to Bill Orrum, and where Cary had found the paper.

"Bring your wagons around and overturn them," Cary told him.

Stockwell raised his hand in a half gesture of protest, but let it fall. He jerked his head at Mullan and they swung back to take over the wagons. Cary retreated to the gate.

Wagon after wagon, they jounced on. If a man focused on them, he could forget that half a nation of Sioux was streaming upon the post. It was a picture Cary would never forget. He would always remember how their horses stifled the bright little stream, and how the horde of them shook out over the meadow like an Indian blanket. He would remember the broken whooping as their hands slapped their mouths. He would remember the way eight hundred running horses jarred the ground, the sensation that he was standing beneath a cliff, waiting for it to crumble upon him.

A little flight of arrows fluttered across the sky and dropped among the teams jamming the gate. An ox twisted to stare, white-eyed, at the feathered wand trembling in its side. The team wedged crosswise in the sally port.

Cary saw the bullwhacker drop from his wagon and try to force his way through the gate into the fort. He slashed at his face with his Stetson. "Cut that bull loose and get your wagon inside!"

He dismounted to throw off the oxbow. They wrestled the animal out of the team. The wagons lunged on. Remounting, Cary saw that the bulk of Stockwell's line had formed raggedly in a flat crescent. Beyond, a trio of muleskinners who had abandoned their wagons in the stream was sprinting for the post. A warrior in advance of the others rode alongside and sank a war axe in a teamster's head.

Through the turmoil of dumped freight and overturned wagons, the final wagon of Cary's string wallowed into the passageway. Above him, he heard the first crashing volley of fire from the walls. He vaulted into his saddle and loped out.

"All right . . . bring them in!"

Stockwell shouted the word to his teamsters. Snatching up horns and rifles, they sprinted for the fort.

VI

The passage strangled with the reek of rifles, long rays of sunlight coasting goldenly through the dust and smoke. Four of the post workers were hauling the gates to. Cary and three others waited, rifles to shoulder, for the last stragglers to sprawl inside. A hundred feet out, a shirtless muleskinner sprawled. A dozen Sioux rushed over him, mounted warriors streaked with yellow, black, and vermilion. An arrow slanted in and lay in the dust of the tunnel.

The gates shouldered together. A moment later a thudding force piled against the logs. There was a high and muted fury from many throats. A salvo of rifle fire rippled from the blockhouses. The thudding finished. Someone with his mouth against the gate began to moan.

They retreated, barring the inner gate. The post had come wildly to life. Wagons and bull teams surged in dusty turmoil. Bullwhackers dragging long Plains rifles clambered to the roofs of buildings. The forward blockhouse rocked with gunfire. A man on the catwalk below the grayed teeth of the wall sprinted low with a keg of black powder in his arms.

In all this hash of confused men and deserted animals, Cary

glimpsed one man standing solemnly near the gate with a carbine crooked in his elbow and his hat on the back of his head, soberly inspecting the pageant. Donovan had a smut of powder across his forehead. Sam abandoned his horse in the corral and swung to Donovan.

"Are you in this?"

"That gate won't hold long." Donovan said.

"It won't have to. They won't get past the outer one. Get up there to the blockhouse and take over. I'll send up the Springfields."

The chaos of firing swelled again, smoke eddying from the tall slots of the blockhouses. A low, insistent thunder spoke of a battering ram against the gate. On the wall, ramrods rose and fell.

Silvertooth was fighting to get the teams corralled, his voice complaining in bitter baritone curses. Cary thrust through the log jam of tall wheels and weathered boxes, sorting among them until he found the arms wagon. He gathered a crew to open the chests and carry armloads of greasy Springfields to the catwalk. He caught a case under his arm and ran to a building wedged into the southwest corner of the walls. Atop the married men's quarters, four men lay in an acrid fume of smoke, loading, ramming, firing.

Cary sprawled among them. He pressed his cheek to a rifle loop and peered down. The horde of Sioux milling before the gate had swelled. The gate was bowing to the very weight of greasy flesh. In the thickening dusk, two or three hundred warriors fired up at the walls, while others hammered at the gate with cottonwood logs. The main force still lingered behind the wagon boxes of Stockwell's ruined train, waiting for the rush when the gate went down. Their muskets flashed, flights of arrows soared into the fort, knuckles thudded red war drums.

Cary nudged the barrel of the Henry into the loophole. A

ball smacked close beside it, fanning yellow splinters over the opening. In that dusty turmoil of warriors, he looked for Esconella's white ghost shirt, the clay-whitened doeskin tunic said to be proof against bullets. But the war chief was back in the trees.

He gouged sixteen .44 balls into the horde of warriors, and sat back to fill the tube. A rifleman jolted off a shot and turned to grope for a shell. He ejected the smoking copper case and slipped a new cartridge home, and then in sober amazement looked at Cary.

"Greased lightnin'?" he said.

The firing fattened, as other Springfields came into action. Wounded warriors dragged themselves away from the walk; a gang of Tetons carried a wounded chief back to the wagons. Horses were down and others pitched wildly through the bitter twilight of black powder smoke. The attack slowly slackened for lack of impetus.

The firing from the walls subsided. The Indians had given back. Single shots rang through the smoke drifting from the walls. Donovan's voice mounted peremptorily.

"Doctor Merritt! A man's wounded up here."

Somewhere in the gray dusk, the envoy called: "I'm coming, man!"

Cary slumped back and could not ease the crabbed grip of tension.

Dusk flooded Young Woman Valley. A rusty green stained the sky above the marbled Bighorns. From the litter of wagons, hissing swarms of arrows arched; rifle fire crusted along the ground and winked out.

Dark came on. The angry legion began to work into bivouacs, warriors from each tribe and village guarding their identity. Fires blinked, glistening bodies slipped back and forth, working up to a dance. Skin rattles shook. Through a fiber of writhing bodies, Cary saw something that lay gauntly, pincushioned with arrows—one of the muleskinners who had not made it to the fort.

He smoked a pipe, glancing from time to time toward the creek. A faint fog of stars misted the sky. At 8:00 he shoved himself up. He struck the pipe against his hand.

"Four-hour watches," he said. "They won't attack tonight, but they'll be crawling up for the dead and wounded. Let them have them. It may be all they'll want. But if they get too thick, watch out."

He descended from the wall. A cramped little city, the post lay in a silent paralysis. He opened the door of the mess shack and shouted for the cooks. He had coffee and venison put on for half the crew, and then strode along the wall, calling men down.

In the forward blockhouse, he found Merritt finishing with the wounded muleskinner. A red stain drenched the linsey-woolsey of the man's right thigh. "We'll carry him to the powder magazine," Merritt said. "It will do for a field hospital."

Cary went ahead. He sounded the signal on the thick portal. A small stone cell, the magazine was buried to half its depth in the earth. After a moment the door opened an inch and a gun muzzle gleamed darkly. Then Gaybird cried out and let Sam push the door open.

Dale Merritt crowded through to clutch the doctor. Ignoring her, Merritt directed the litter-bearers inside. "They've pulled off for the night," Cary said.

Dale turned quickly. "But surely they won't attack again? Haven't they had enough?"

"Jericho had walls, too," said Cary. "You ladies can sleep in your rooms tonight, but you'll come back here at four o'clock. Food will be ready in a few minutes."

Daniel Edge walked to the mess with Sam and Gaybird. He

wiped his mouth on his sleeve, an overly heavy man with a sea walk. "The Pilgrims never had it harder," he said bitterly.

Sam and Gaybird sat across a long table from each other. A distant surf sounded in Cary's ears, remnant of the firing. Gaybird was soberly occupied with her thoughts.

"Tell me about Crazy Dog," she said finally.

"I'd rather tell you about a girl I know."

"Would I like her?"

"She's a hummingbird in armor. Even a thousand Sioux can't upset her."

Her chin began to tremble then. "You'd better tell me about Crazy Dog," she said.

"The chief's going to walk. Merritt took a bullet out of him."

"And he'll come to Laramie for the parley?"

"He said he'd be there."

"Then there's still some chance. . . ."

A rifle exploded in the night—and echoes cascaded through the post. It was silent again. The Pawnee cook brought steaks and coffee. Sam regarded Gaybird with a sober smile. "Will it be worth it? We may never see the time when you can ride out without wondering what's behind the next ridge. Will anything be worth that?"

"I've never seen it any other way," she declared slowly, "and it's always been worth it."

Afterward, with Gaybird in her own room behind the commissary, Cary made a slow tour of the post. It was now past 10:00. Each roof had its silent watchers. The blockhouses had their sharpshooters who smoked quietly with rifles across their knees. He mounted the wall. In the forward blockhouse the smoky darkness was restless with low talk and snoring. Shells and burned primers *crunched* under his boots as he crossed the floor. He kicked a bucket of water, and swore under his breath. The air was choked with tobacco fumes. He put his palms against the wall and peered through a slot.

He thought he saw a wagon moving. He heard Donovan growl: "They've pulled away half their dead. They may quit when they git 'em all."

"Keep thinking it, if you want. It's as good a prayer as any."

Coy Mullan's voice said testily: "I never seen the Injun yet that liked climbing while he was being shot at."

Cary put his back to the wall, thinking about the wagon. "We can't shoot at a thousand of them at once, if they swarm together."

"What'll they climb on? Ladders?"

"No," Cary said. "Wagons."

The blockhouse was quiet. Someone grunted and shifted his position, and a muleskinner growled: "Wagons. Yes. That'd be the caper."

Mullan rose from a corner and stood by the trap door. He was silent a moment. He said roughly: "I'll go down and have a bait. When you've time, Cary, I want a talk with you."

You want to tell me it was all Stockwell's fault about the rifles, Cary said to himself. *You didn't know he was planning it, until it was too late. I know the story.* "When I've got time," he said, "will be when the Sioux have left. Send up a bucket of coffee."

Reliefs came. Carrying their rifles, the men descended the ladder. A last man slouched in beside Cary as he stepped onto the catwalk.

"We did have a date at Fort Graybull, didn't we?" said Donovan. "This is Graybull, now, eh?"

"We did have."

"There's been times you were thirty seconds from a ball in the back. That's happened in the Army. Only I fight from the front. Why did you think you could handle me like a greenhorn?"

"One of us," Cary said, "had to handle the other. You'd have been handling me before we reached Fort Reno. It's a point with you not to be handled by anybody. You must have gone crazy in the Army."

". . . I bought out after six months. Then, my God, ran into you. Was it any business of yours how I drank and worked, so long as I got my chores done?"

"There's only one commodity I can make money out of," Sam told him. "Men. All the trade goods in Wyoming won't do me any good if I can't move my wagons. Some men can pack goods with less loss than others, and now and then a man can pack a wagon, whack bulls, and fight Indians, too. I don't know why I picked you for one of those. Silvertooth told me I was crazy. I picked you the way I'd pick a horse . . . with the heart more than the head."

"What do you like in a work horse?"

"Something that doesn't fight the bit. You fight the bit because you think discipline is beneath you. Donovan, it isn't beneath anybody. The sergeants you fought with were under discipline to the shavetails. The shavetails answered to the captains, and back in Washington there's a general with poor digestion who's under discipline to every man and woman in the country."

Donovan peered solemnly into Cary's eyes as though to be sure he was not being joshed. He asked scoffingly: "Who do you answer to?"

"To you. And to all the other men I'm supposed to move through hell without getting the smell of fire on them."

Donovan shifted his rifle. He looked down suddenly. He muttered: "Well, that's one way of looking at it. . . ." Solemnly he went down the ladder.

Cary remained in the blockhouse until 3:30, sleeping a little. There was the depressing air of an Army hospital ward. Most of the men lay on the floor, turning much and sleeping little, their breathing heavy. A teamster startled them all by coming out of a nightmare with a yell and lunging to his feet. Someone threw a dipper of water on him and he sank down, shaken.

Dawn would begin about 4:30. One hour. Cary checked the ammunition, took a last look at the Sioux camp, and sensed a throb of movement in it. He left John Silvertooth in charge and went down to rouse all the relief men.

As he descended the ladder, a rifle shot tore the pre-dawn silence. He stared at the corrals, from which the shot had come. A sentry shouted and there was a bristling of guards along the walls. But in a moment someone called: "Go back to sleep! Owls ought to know better than to roost on walls anyway!"

The man sauntered from the rear of a storehouse that backed up to the corral. He halted, leaning against the poles, and ejected a shell from his rifle. Cary moved from the ladder and went along the corral fence until he reached the man. It was Mark Stockwell.

Stockwell slowly thrust the bolt of his rifle forward and they regarded each other in the tingling gray of early dawn. "Won't be long now," said the Montanan. "I wonder how much of my freight will be left?"

"It doesn't seem to worry me," Cary said.

". . . You're nursing your suspicions for all they're worth, aren't you?"

"Found a hole to crawl through?" Cary asked. He saw him clearly—saw the tough, aggressive mind that would wriggle out of any trap. He was a nice balance of greed, lack of squeamishness, and egotism—the kind of far-sighted egotism that sometimes got a man's profile on a coin or a postage stamp, and sometimes got him hanged.

Stockwell said: "Orrum was a damned fool. I warned him against leaving the train, but he was in a hurry to see that French girl of his in Butte. He had a load of old Harper's Ferrys I was buying from him. I dickered for your Springfields once, too,

197

remember? I told him to leave them at the post and my manager would pay him." Cary did not reply. Stockwell stirred under his regard and demanded testily: "Well, what did you think?"

"You know what I think. I mean to put you in the guardhouse when we get through this. You'll go back to Cheyenne in irons. You can handle your own men better than I can or I'd have locked you up before now. And we need your gun. We need every gun, to match the ones you put in their hands."

Stockwell said: "I'd like to see any ten of you put me in irons."

"You will."

Cary walked away from him. At the rear blockhouse he made his inspection. He located Donovan in the mess hall. He sat down across from him with a mug of coffee. Donovan's eyes nestled in tired, puckered flesh. His face was surly, as a good foot soldier's should have been.

"I'm going to leave you in charge of the yard," Cary stated. "I want the freight dumped from eight or ten of the wagons and a barricade made out of the boxes. Lay them out to face the gate."

"What makes you think they'll come in that way?"

"Because, if they start moving wagons up to the walls, I'll open the gates."

Donovan pressed his fingers against his eyes. "I'm tired. I don't hear things right. You said . . . ?"

"I'll open the gates. Let them in. If they storm us at too many points, we can't stop them. They'll be all over the post, setting fires."

"And how in thunder do you think you're going to stop eight hundred at one spot?"

"With fire power. It's the only way we can hope to. You don't have to kill every man in an army to lick it. If we can pile them up shoulder deep at the entrance, the others are going to lose heart. Especially if we can make a liar out of Esconella, with his bulletproof ghost shirt."

"Let them in," Donovan muttered, peering darkly down into his coffee cup.

Cary rose from the bench. "Maybe we won't have to. But if we do, I want the wagons ready."

A rifle roared. Another hammered out its horde of echoes, then a crackling of shots from the south wall broke out. Cary shouted to the room: "Get to your posts!"

Outside, a murky light seeped from the sky. Tongues of fire licked through a slot in the forward blockhouse. A guard bawled: "They're bringing up the wagons! Let's have some of you coffee-swillers up here . . . !"

Cary went back to the rear blockhouse. From the ladder, he looked down to see Donovan impressing teamsters into service. A man shook off his hand. Donovan struck him with the back of his fist and sent him reeling toward the wagons. Cary climbed into the dim reek of powder smoke.

The dregs of night lay over the fields. Through river mist he discerned the gaunt shapes of freight wagons moving down both sides of the post. One was already against the sally port. There was no evidence of bull teams. A dozen Sioux could push a wagon without difficulty, lurking on the off side so that they were protected from rifle fire. Yet the main horde of Ogallala, Brûlé, and Hunkpapa warriors remained among the vestiges of Stockwell's freight.

Rifle fire rippled up and down the walls. The wagons came on, ghost-like in the dawn. Inside the post, a wagon went over with a splintering crash. Cary turned to study the yard. One or two wagons had been unloaded and moved into place about fifty feet from the inner gate of the sally port. Donovan had now given up unloading them and his workmen were pushing them into place loaded and overturning them with a bull team.

Cary turned to Silvertooth. "Take over the walls, John. Hold the men as they are until the attack begins. I figure it will be at the main gate. When it comes, take most of the men to the front and pour it into them."

Crusty with fatigue and tension, Silvertooth growled: "You seem damned sure they'll play it your way."

"I aim to make it so attractive they can't pass it up. What's more tempting than an open gate? But we knock them over as they come through."

"And what's more suspicious? Esconella's a fox, not a fool. Sometimes I think you're crazy!"

"This is going to be convincing."

He descended the ladder and slung off to the rear posts to pass the word. Oxen and horses surged anxiously about the corral as he strode by.

He headed for the rear posts, but in the shadows back of the commissary he stumbled over something. He caught himself and looked back. Puzzled, he returned to the man who lay against the log wall. This man's cheek was against the earth. His arms were drawn under him and one leg was pulled up. Cary pulled him onto his back. Coy Mullan looked up at him with filmy blue eyes. His throat had been torn by a bullet and there was a grisly display of cords and muscles. He hoarded something in his hand—a clutch of buckskin whangs, a handful of fringe torn from the yoke of someone's shirt. Cary regarded him grimly. *Owls ought to know better than to roost on trading post walls, and wagon masters should know enough not to question their employer's motives.* Coy Mullan had learned this too late. . . .

A man of ideas, Donovan had placed crates of hardware in random fashion just within the inner gate. The warriors who rushed through it would not come on a straight line. Their charge would be slowed and blunted. Cary made a hand, helping to overturn the wagons. Between the boxes they threw up a shallow earthworks. A pattern grew—a wide half wheel of wagon boxes confronting the gate, crates radiating from the hub like stub ends of sunken piles. A second, paralleling ring of boxes began thirty feet behind the first, the final firing line.

Crates of shells were split open and scattered for ready loading. Cary was sweating. He came face to face with the question of whether he had forgotten anything, any *pons asinorum* of military strategy that might suddenly backlash on him.

Donovan was manning the boxes with teamsters as fast as the wagons were overturned. Axes made rough loopholes in the bottoms of the boxes. As Cary brought up a crate of shells, Donovan growled: "I'd like to meet the fella who said Injuns don't besiege."

"After today, maybe he'll be right. Or it might be that white men won't build forts any more. You'll stay with the second rank. Pick off any who get past us, and move over if we have to pull back."

He found Daniel Edge.

"Dan, I've a chore for you."

Edge blinked slowly and pulled a forearm across his forehead. "I know. I reckon that's what I get for bein' fat."

"That's what you get for being fat and trustworthy. You won't go soft?"

"God keep me from it. And God help all of us, Sam."

Edge labored slowly past the commissary toward the powder magazine. Sam saw him pat his shirt pocket, like a man leaving on a scout who checks to see whether he has his matches.

She came to him then in a little cameo of vision, smiling and sweet, sitting on a wagon tongue as she brushed her blue-black hair. It struck him bitterly that nothing should be so hard as this, nothing so lonely and full of consequences.

And now Silvertooth came to the window of the forward blockhouse and roared down: "Something's up! Esconella's ranging up and down the line! Make your play, if you're going to!"

The darkness of the powder magazine was warm and thick as smoke. Gaybird sat on a pallet against the wall, a bucket of water where she could reach it at her right, a rifle on her lap, the wounded man at her left. There was an odor of sickness and medicines. That, and the monotonous, snoring moans the man made, burdened the darkness.

It was tiring to have the eyes opened, focused on nothing. It was more tiring to squeeze them shut. While she sat there, she worked on knitting she had brought from her wagon. Her needles made a tiny, good-natured prattle. Sound suddenly pricked through the stone walls, like a distant crackling of flames. Gaybird's heart compressed.

There was a scratching sound and light broke dazzlingly in the room. Dale Merritt was on her knees a few feet away, holding a dripping wax match in her fingers.

"I won't sit in the darkness like . . . like a criminal waiting to be executed!" she cried. "Why did they have to put this man in with us? Why . . . ?"

Gaybird said firmly: "Put the match out!" She was not looking at Dale, but at the crates and kegs of shells and powder.

Dale struggled up. "I'll not put it out! If we've got to stay here, I'll know whether it's rats or Indians I hear!"

She faced Gaybird furiously. Gaybird quietly raised a dipper of water from the bucket and hurled it. The light was extinguished. Dale began to sob.

"Just sit down," Gaybird told her, "and think less of us and more of them out there. That isn't so nice, what they're doing. Much less nice than waiting."

At the same time, she was not so sure. Now that the rifle fire was a full-throated roaring, she had to cease knitting. Her fingers were unsteady. The wounded man began to mouth a word, over and over. She gave him water.

Then she sat back and thought of Sam. She wished she had done one thing last night—given him the ring and asked him to put it on her finger. But it had all been too confused for sentiment, and now, perhaps, he might never do it.

Dale was whispering: "But they can't get in, can they?"

"I don't know. I don't think so."

"If they do, what will happen? I mean . . . what do they do to . . . to women?"

"Sometimes they make slaves of them. They don't covet us as one might think. They have contempt for white flesh."

The strong-hearted lie. What did the braves do? And what did the squaws do, drunk on jealousy and cruelty? She was not sure, because men did not tell such things to women.

The door sounded to the signal knock. Quickly she crossed the dark floor to open it. The cold, gray dawn seeped in. Fat Daniel Edge stood there, smiling, a short axe in his hand.

"Ladies," he said heartily, "we thought you might be wanting company. I see you brought your knitting, Gaybird. Sam said to be sure you put heels in his socks this time. You left them off, last time, you remember." Dan's smile grew broader.

He came in, closing the door on the shocking thunder of the rifles. They heard him cross the floor toward the powder kegs. The axe made a single, sharp smack against a keg, and a piece of wood fell to the floor.

Dale said hastily: "You may sit over here by me, if you want, Mister Edge. There's a pallet."

Dan Edge seemed to yawn. "No, I'll be quite well right here." He made himself comfortable on the split-open top of the powder keg.

Cary took his horse from the line and loped through the wagons, striking Donovan on the back as he passed. He found Tom Kane, the scout, and shouted: "Come along!"

The gate bars were dressed eight-by-eights. The two men lifted them out of the iron hasps. The gate swung slowly outward. Cary mounted again and looked out. He had again the feeling that the dammed-up fury of the wilderness must rush into this gap, forcing it like a hole in a dike. In the gray dawn, he witnessed the pre-attack skirmishing of the Sioux, the little pointless rushes, the rattled weapons and curveting ponies, which corresponded to a white man's spitting on his palms and settling down to work. He heard their sharp animal yelping. Esconella, distinctive in his famed white ghost shirt, a red blanket across his lap as he sat his pony, had discovered the open gate. He sat utterly still.

Between the gate and the wagons lay the body of the murdered teamster. He was naked, and bristled with arrows. Cary said to Kane: "Back away, now, and get to your post. Let the first man through . . . it had better be me."

He spurred the horse out of the post and crossed the torn, bloody ground before the gate. The silence of the walls ached in his ears. He loped for the corpse of the muleskinner. Reaching it, he swung his pony broadside to the Indians and slid off on the post side. He crouched beside the dead man, not touching him, not looking at him. There was nothing he could do for the dead man, but there might be something the muleskinner could do for him. Recovering your dead—there was something an Indian could understand.

Then a yell like the scream of a mountain lion came from a bronze throat. A gun *cracked*. Peering under the barrel of the horse, Cary saw the line begin to melt toward him. Ponies and mounted warriors oozed through gaps in the wagons. Clots of horsemen flowed around the ends. The wilderness had found the hole in the dike.

Cary lunged for the pony. With his hand on the saddle horn, he felt it quiver. He heard the *pop* of an arrow entering the tough little body. The horse sank down, biting at the feathered shaft in its side. Cary turned to run.

The Springfields began to shout, throwing out dirty-black smoke and shuddering explosions. It seemed, at that moment, that all hell had broken loose.

Behind him, the line was shredding, the faster ponies racing ahead of the others. As he reached the gate, he turned to raise his carbine. A breechclouted warrior carrying a musket and a bull-hide shield led the pack. Sam put him on the tip of the Henry and fired. He felt the quivering of earth under the horses' hoofs, and, just as he turned into the gate, he saw the Sioux throw his hands up and leave the wooden saddle.

Cary ran through the deserted sally port and entered the post. Crates studded the ground like stumps. He dodged through them to the first line of wagon boxes. He sprawled behind a box and came into a kneeling position with one foot kinked under him. He raised his gun to steady it against the gray wood of the tailgate. He was gasping for breath. His hand pulled at the loading lever, inching it down, thrusting it back, until angrily he smacked it home and circled his finger through the trigger guard.

There was the *boom* and echo of rifles along the catwalk. Riflemen jolted to the kick of the guns. Suddenly a man ran from the forward blockhouse and came halfway down the steps, to sit down and wait, his rifle trained on the crates.

The flat hammering of pony hoofs filled the passage. An Indian was shouting soprano invective. The sally port seemed gagging on its gorge of oncoming Indians and horses.

A naked Sioux with rifle and reins in his left hand and a coup stick raised in his right lunged out of the passage. The teamster on the steps got his shot in an instant ahead of the others. The

205

Sioux dropped the rifle. The other balls struck him simultaneously, changing the look of his face and breast. His pony swerved and kicked out at a crate. The next horse ran broadside into him. A rifleman knocked its rider onto the ground.

It was suddenly as if a dam had broken. Cary felt his body know itself. He was in the path of a flood. It boiled with a flotsam of horsehide, of copper skin streaked blue and red and green. Lances, bows, and rifles tossed and thrummed and roared.

He found himself firing. A hot shell stung his cheek. A hand that did not seem to be his slapped the loading lever down and up. He was firing into the howling vortex of ponies and riders. The quadrangle was choking on them: scores—hundreds you could not fail to hit.

A splatter of color broke off and bubbled through the boxes, getting behind his wagon. A half-dozen Sioux had broken the first line of defense. They swung and charged back, and one of them fired a musket and a man was shouting: "My arm, my arm!"

Bullwhackers were sprawling everywhere and their shots were a stuttering clap of thunder. There was not an Indian on his pony an instant after the six broke through. Someone flopped onto a scrambling brave and a skinning knife fell.

Cary's eyes lingered on a gray stone structure beyond all this, tucked in behind a building at the rear—the powder magazine. *I hope she can't hear. I don't want her to have it to remember. And yet she must remember, she must be able to look back on this day. It will not all end for her before the sun climbs the wall.*

He looked back. Another dozen Indians could not be packed into that shouting square. Crates were overturned and spilled. Blankets, white crockery, and jugs of vinegar tangled the ponies' hoofs. Horses lay on their backs, screaming and kicking at the air. A bitter smoke wound through the buildings. The fort was a travail of the dying.

The cauldron was filled. The pressure in back was greater than the restraint of the wagon boxes and rifles, and in an instant it would boil over on the riflemen.

Cary lurched up, shouting: "Back up! Keep firing!"

They gave back stubbornly. Some of Donovan's men retreated to the porch of the commissary. A tall Ogallala with an eagle bone through his topknot and a knife in his teeth rushed a teamster. A double-bitted axe met him. The Indian went down in a full run.

Hunched behind the box, Cary reloaded the Henry. He raised it again and dully chose a target. Then something in the crowd of warriors screamed for his attention.

"There he is!" Cary yelled. Clay-whitened, its stippling of blue porcupine quills just visible, Esconella's ghost shirt was struggling forward. A lance flashed, fluttering a fresh scalp as the point came down into the body of a teamster caught in the muck of Indians. Then the shirt again came ahead, twisting through the mob, seeming truly to be magic. Rising slowly, Cary went to meet it.

Esconella guided his horse with his knees. He held the lance high, blood dripping from the point. Arrogance burned in his face. *This is his day,* Cary thought, his hour. *The first war chief to overpower a fort!* Across his face yellow-and-black bars shone greasily. His eyes found Cary, standing beside the wagon box. The moccasined heels struck the pony's ribs. He leaned forward, his arm carrying the lance back.

Cary raised the carbine and pulled the trigger. The hammer fell without a sound. He looked dumbly at the gun. Empty. He swore and dropped it, reaching blindly for his Colt, but Esconella was over him, driving the lance in. He felt the point tug at his armpit and go through his shirt. Something sleek and sharp slid across his ribs. His hands closed on the shaft of the lance. He hauled back and the Sioux released it. The lance fell. Esconella reached for his revolver—Bill Orrum's Colt—but Cary was lunging in to seize the Indian's leg and drag him out of the saddle. The Roman-nosed warrior was on top of him as they went down.

They were on the ground. Cary's hand closed on the rancid mat of hair. He held the lean head down and rolled over to pin the twisting body with his own. Gory fingers closed on his throat. His free hand groped at his hip, searching. Now it closed on a smooth, corrugated cylinder of bone and he pulled his case knife free. He let Esconella see the knife. He felt the fingers leave his throat, and drove quickly. The knife struck Esconella's collar bone; it slanted off into his throat. Sam struck again, and a third time.

He stood up and dragged the chief's body behind the wagon. He cut the bloody shirt from it and found a discarded rifle to hang it on. Jamming the gun between the spokes of a wheel, he let the shirt dangle where the Sioux could see it.

Up on the catwalk there was a wild yelling. The old, primitive story was still good business, Cary reckoned. Chief slaying chief.

A brave discerned the shirt and rode forward to recover it. Bullets began to hit him; he kept coming, but within reach of it a final ball slugged him aside. He was down in the roil of hoofs and dust.

Heated to smoking, the Springfields still rammed their machine-made bullets out; the queer bolts lifted and the copper shells slid home, and chunks of .50-caliber lead roared out in a fog of brackish smoke. It was coming home to the Sioux. These were fifty men with the firepower of two hundred. Esconella had lied to them. There was no magic in his deerskin tunic. There was no wisdom in his strategy.

Cary saw the beginning of the pressing back. With a full magazine, he stepped into the interval between the rings of wagon boxes and commenced firing. Sweat trickled saltily onto his lips. This was a cow-pen slaughter. They were not fighting. They were running, riding, crawling—back to the sally port. There they ran into the glut of braves still dreaming of scalps and high deeds.

Cary brought the rifle up again and frowned across the sights. Indians did not comprehend surrender, but they understood retreat. You retreated when the hearts of your gods turned bad. You retreated when you had to climb the backs of your own butchered companions to get at the enemy. Nearest the gate, the bucks fought back into the passage. Among the wagon boxes, marooned warriors battled with clubbed rifles and broken lances. It was a massacre from mythology.

Cary had had enough. He raised his arm. "Hold your fire!"

But no one heard him. The rifles continued to roar. Men continued to fight. Men continued to die.

The eternal sun came up, as if reluctantly, to peer through the smoke and dust. A torpid reaction had rotted the life of the post after the retreat. Across Young Woman Creek, a mauled army of Sioux lurked among the trees, waiting for nightfall, when they could recover their dead. If the white man comprehended the etiquette of warfare, he would place the dead and wounded on the ground before the post.

Gray with powder grime, Cary saw to the caring-for of the wounded and tolled off a dozen men to carry the dead outside. As the wounded were cared for, they were laid beside the dead.

He remembered Coy Mullan. Now that significance came back to such small things as a single murdered wagon master, he remembered Mullan. . . . He had seen Mark Stockwell helping to carry a wounded bullwhacker into the dispensary, but he had not seen him since.

Cary went past the commissary and turned into the alley between the long building and a storehouse. A cold night gloom clung close to the ground. He saw Mullan's body. Pressed against the unbarked log of the commissary was another figure. He drew his Colt. The man held Mullan's right hand in both of his, but he dropped it quickly and rose to his feet.

They were face to face, fifteen feet apart. Stockwell was a gray, hunched figure without a hat. He made a hopeless gesture.

"Done for Coy, they did," he said. "Shot in the throat."

"Yes, before the fight started," Cary said. "I saw the fringe in his hand. You should have come back for it before his fingers froze."

Stockwell moved away from the wall. A dark gleam of metal showed the upward movement of his hand.

In the alley there was one great throb of sound, a single, stunning heartbeat. Then sound flowed out both ends of it and Cary was alone with a man who lounged woodenly against the wall, and dropped his gun, and sank to his knees.

Darkness came down Young Woman Creek and shapes moved on the meadow. Pickets observed them from the walls. In the dispensary, someone lighted a lamp. Dr. Merritt had been asleep with his head on the table. He looked up to see his wife placing the lamp before him. She appeared very thin and pinched, but she had brushed her hair and changed her gown. She came across the scrubbed, wet floor.

"Asa, you must come to bed. You're exhausted."

He shook his head. "Dead."

"We have a nice room next to Mister Edge's. I have some marvelous beef broth for you . . . and real coffee!"

Merritt leaned forward; he looked as though he were falling out of the chair. But he put his palms on his knees and slowly levered himself onto his feet. "All I want is sleep. All I'll ever want. I've been riding or fighting or doing surgery for . . . how long? Two days. That's a long time for a little Washington politician."

She held his arm and smiled at him, more in coaxing than in persuasion. "And still, we had good times in Washington, didn't we?" she said. "And we shall have again. It's all very well to be patriotic, but we've earned something better than Wyoming. We're going home, Asa!"

He was silent, looking about the cramped little chamber. Behind this small surgery was the infirmary; he would be back here a dozen times tonight. Yet there was a species of comfort in the thought. These men, when they summoned him, were a continent removed from dissimulation. When they said—*I need you.*—they meant it.

"I won't go back to Washington," he said. "I'll send my report from Fort Russell."

Dale's hands dropped away. She looked at him like a child meeting punishment. "You'll go back to your practice?"

"I am thinking," Merritt said, "of contracting to the Army. There are forts in this country without a single surgeon."

Men were coming across the ground from the commissary. Someone spoke drunkenly and dragged his feet.

Dale's lips parted. Her face grew lax and her hands clenched.

Merritt stood up, smiling. "If it's prestige you want, my dear, I'll be the most important man on the post. I'll wear a uniform. You'll be Missus Doctor Merritt, and no officer's lady would dare give a tea without inviting you."

Two men ascended the steps and crossed the porch with a third man half carried between them. It was Tom Kane, the scout. Kane's face had been mauled. All three of these men gave off vapors of whiskey.

"A little disagreement," said one of the teamsters. He helped seat Kane on the table. "This fella was recruiting a company to mine gold. He tried to get Donovan to make a hand, and Donovan whipped him. He promised the same to any other man who tried to leave before the end of the season. Funny thing because Donovan was only drinking beer."

"Not so funny," the doctor murmured.

After he had pulled together a cut in the man's eyebrow and mended his lip, he let him go. They heard the trio leave; then the doctor backed down the flame of the lamp, left it on the table, and took his wife's arm. She did not move. Merritt regarded her and said gently: "Of course I wouldn't make you stay. If you don't happen to like this country, nothing can make you."

Something about her at that instant—some softness of indecision—made him think of the first year of their marriage. Dependency in a woman was a fine thing.

"Do you want me to go back?" she asked him.

Merritt held her hands, slowly shaking his head. "I think you know what I want you to do."

Dale came against him and began to weep.

It was late when Gaybird found Sam in the armory.

Now he was fitting the Springfields into wall racks, except for a few chests stored against the wall. The stocks had been rubbed with linseed oil and the browned steel had a moist luster.

"I think you're in love with them," she said.

Cary padlocked the retainer and dropped the key in his pocket. "I brought them up here to sell," he said, "but I'll hang onto them now until the Army comes back. That may not be long." She watched him move cases of ammunition about. He frowned over the arrangement. "Maybe those ought to go into the powder magazine."

"I'm sure I wouldn't know," she said.

Cary saw, without appearing to, that she wore the candy-striped gown she had worn in Cheyenne. It gave her the silhouette of a hand bell, a slender stem above, a generous flair from the waist, her slippers just visible. She wore a narrow blue sash and a velvet wristband, and he detected a richer scent than the decorous rose-water fragrance he associated with her, an out-and-out French perfume.

He set one case atop another. "I was worried that there might be rats down there this morning."

"No," she said.

He inspected a gun crate, saying gruffly: "These will have to be nailed down against the dust." Her slippers were silent on the floor, but her dress and petticoats rustled tartly, and just as she reached the door Sam said: "You've put your hair up."

She turned. Her chin was up as well as her hair. "Braids are for girls," she said.

Sam went to her. "And is there anything wrong with girls?"

"Some people seem to think so."

He reached up and found the bone hairpins that made a coronet of her rich, dark braids. He drew them out and let the braids fall forward over her shoulders. He ran his hands down them. "That's it! You looked like a business partner that way. . . . I almost forgot to tell you about the upstairs room your father had," he said.

"I suppose there are guns stored in it, too?" A smile brushed her lips.

"Guns? There's a new goose-feather mattress on the bed and a crockery bowl and pitcher. I put down some Indian rugs last spring."

"Well, that's nice," she said. "For you?"

"For us," Sam said.

Gaybird bit her lip. Sam picked her up, the silken, rustling froth of her skirts billowing about them. She was pulling something from the bosom of her dress, reproving him: "Sam! This is indecent. There!" She put the ring in his hand.

Cary laced the ring carefully over her finger. "Didn't I do this once before?"

"But you didn't finish the ceremony. You didn't kiss me."

He kissed her, swaying slightly, their eyes closed. She took a deep, trembling breath when his face moved away. Sam reached for the wall lamp without taking his eyes from her, and, holding it by the ring, he carried her into the dark vestibule.

ACKNOWLEDGMENTS

"Brand of the Bear Flag Mutineers" first appeared in *Star Western* (4/45). Copyright © 1945 by Popular Publications, Inc. Copyright © renewed 1973 by Frank Bonham. Copyright © 2009 by David Bonham for restored material.

"The Dark Border" first appeared under the title "Sons of the Back-Shoot Border" in *Star Western* (8/48). Copyright © 1948 by Popular Publications, Inc. Copyright © renewed 1976 by Frank Bonham. Copyright © 2009 by David Bonham for restored material.

"Chivaree" first appeared under the title "Lovely Little Liar" in *Star Western* (4/51). Copyright © 1951 by Popular Publications, Inc. Copyright © renewed 1979 by Frank Bonham. Copyright © 2009 by David Bonham for restored material.

"Blood on The Bozeman Trail" first appeared under the title "That Bloody Bozeman Trail" in *Dime Western* (6/50). Copyright © 1950 by Popular Publications, Inc. Copyright © renewed 1978 by Frank Bonham. Copyright © 2009 by David Bonham for restored material.

ABOUT THE AUTHOR

Frank Bonham in a career that spanned five decades achieved excellence as a noted author of young adult fiction and detective and mystery fiction, as well as making significant contributions to Western fiction. By 1941 his fiction was already headlining Street and Smith's *Western Story* and by the end of the decade his Western novels were being serialized in *The Saturday Evening Post*. His first Western, Lost Stage Valley (1948), was purchased as the basis for the motion picture, *Stage to Tucson* (Columbia, 1951) with Rod Cameron as Grif Holbrook and Sally Eilers as Annie Benson. "I have tried to avoid," Bonham once confessed, "the conventional cowboy story, but I think it was probably a mistake. That is like trying to avoid crime in writing a mystery book. I just happened to be more interested in stagecoaching, mining, railroading. . . ." Yet, notwithstanding, it is precisely the interesting—and by comparison with the majority of Western novels—exotic backgrounds of Bonham's novels that give them an added dimension. He was highly knowledgeable in the technical aspects of transportation and communication in the 19th-Century American West. In introducing these backgrounds into his narratives, especially when combined with his firm grasp of idiomatic Spanish spoken by many of his Mexican characters, his stories and novels are elevated to a higher plane in which the historical sense of the period is always very much in the forefront. This historical aspect of his Western fiction early drew accolades from reviewers so that on one occasion the *Long Beach Press Telegram* predicted that "when the time comes to find an author who can best fill the gap in Western fiction left by Ernest Haycox, it may be that Frank Bonham will serve well." Among his best Western novels are *Snaketrack* (1952), *Night Raid* (1954), *The Feud at Spanish Ford* (1954), and *Last Stage West* (1959). *Trouble at Temescal* will be his next Five Star Western.

ABOUT THE EDITOR

Bill Pronzini was born in Petaluma, California. His earliest Western fiction was published under his own name and a variety of pseudonyms in *Zane Grey Western Magazine*. Among his most notable Western novels are *The Last Days of Horse-Shy Halloran* (1987) and *Firewind* (1989). He is also the editor of numerous Western story collections, including *Under the Burning Sun: Western Stories* (Five Star Westerns, 1997) by H.A. DeRosso, *Renegade River: Western Stories* (Five Star Westerns, 1998) by Giff Cheshire, and *Tracks in the Sand* by H.A. DeRosso (Five Star Westerns, 2001). His own Western story collection, *All the Long Years* (Five Star Westerns, 2001), was followed by *Burgade's Crossing* (Five Star Westerns, 2003), *Quincannon's Game* (Five Star Westerns, 2005), and *Coyote and Quarter-Moon* (Five Star Westerns, 2006). His latest Five Star Western is *Crucifixion River* with Marcia Muller. Its original title novella won a Spur Award from the Western Writers of America for the best short fiction of 2007.